The Camper

When a homeless man is found murdered a few blocks from Morgan Beylerian's house in south Seattle, everyone seems to consider the body just so much additional trash to be cleared from the neighborhood. But Morgan liked the guy. They used to chat when Morgan brought Nick groceries once a week.

And the brutal way the man was killed reminds Morgan of their shared Mormon heritage, back when the faithful agreed to have their throats slit if they ever revealed temple secrets.

Did Nick's former wife take action when her ex-husband refused to grant a temple divorce? Did his murder have something to do with the public accusations that brought an end to his promising career?

Morgan does his best to investigate when no one else seems to care, but it isn't easy as a man living paycheck to paycheck himself, only able to pursue his investigation via public transit.

As he continues his search for the killer, Morgan's friends withdraw and his husband threatens to leave. When another homeless man is killed and Morgan is accused of the crime, things look even bleaker.

But his troubles aren't over yet.

Will Morgan find the killer before the killer finds him?

Praise for Johnny Townsend

In *Zombies for Jesus*, "Townsend isn't writing satire, but deeply emotional and revealing portraits of people who are, with a few exceptions, quite lovable."

Kel Munger, *Sacramento News and Review*

In *Sex among the Saints,* "Townsend writes with a deadpan wit and a supple, realistic prose that's full of psychological empathy....he takes his protagonists' moral struggles seriously and invests them with real emotional resonance."

Kirkus Reviews

Let the Faggots Burn: The UpStairs Lounge Fire is "a gripping account of all the horrors that transpired that night, as well as a respectful remembrance of the victims."

Terry Firma, *Patheos*

"Johnny Townsend's 'Partying with St. Roch' [in the anthology *Latter-Gay Saints*] tells a beautiful, haunting tale."

Kent Brintnall, *Out in Print: Queer Book Reviews*

Selling the City of Enoch is "sharply intelligent...pleasingly complex...The stories are full of...doubters, but there's no vindictiveness in these pages; the characters continuously poke holes in Mormonism's more extravagant absurdities, but they take very little pleasure in doing so....Many of Townsend's stories...have a provocative edge to them, but this [book] displays a great deal of insight as well...a playful, biting and surprisingly warm collection."

Kirkus Reviews

Gayrabian Nights is "an allegorical tour de force...a hard-core emotional punch."

Gay. Guy. Reading and Friends

The Washing of Brains has "A lovely writing style, and each story [is] full of unique, engaging characters....immensely entertaining."

Rainbow Awards

In *Dead Mankind Walking*, "Townsend writes in an energetic prose that balances crankiness and humor....A rambunctious volume of short, well-crafted essays..."

Kirkus Reviews

Johnny Townsend

The

Camper Killings

Johnny Townsend

Special thanks to Donna Banta and Robert Ramsay for their editorial assistance

For more of Donna's work,

please read *False Prophet* and *Seer Stone.*

For more of Robert's work,

please read *Wreck of the Royal Express.*

Contents

Chapter One: Blood in the Gutter.................................11
Chapter Two: Blood Down the Aisle...........................25
Chapter Three: Blood from a Stone...........................37
Chapter Four: Man in the Torn, Red Slip.....................46
Chapter Five: Man in the Crotchless, Black Jeans.............58
Chapter Six: Man in the Stained, Blue Sweats.................67
Chapter Seven: Man in the Tattered, Gray Underwear........78
Chapter Eight: A Cackle of Karens............................87
Chapter Nine: A Chaos of Clues...............................98
Chapter Ten: A Cacophony of Creeps.........................109
Chapter Eleven: A Conundrum of Concerns..................117
Chapter Twelve: Treasures We Leave Behind...............127
Chapter Thirteen: Trash We Throw Away....................140
Chapter Fourteen: Trash We Carry with Us..................152
Chapter Fifteen: Treasures We Cling To..................... 164
Chapter Sixteen: Moderation in Excess.......................172
Chapter Seventeen: Loading the Chamber...................179
Chapter Eighteen: Lining up the Sights......................190
Chapter Nineteen: Cocking the Hammer....................200
Chapter Twenty: Pulling the Trigger..........................212
Chapter Twenty-One: Gluttony in Moderation..............223
Books by Johnny Townsend...................................232
What Readers Have Said......................................246

Johnny Townsend

Chapter One: Blood in the Gutter

Blood was dripping from Nick's camper door. I'd promised to bring the man some groceries on my way home from work, but he couldn't be so starved yet he'd passed out and hit his head. No mouse or even rat trap would create that kind of blood spill. And Nick would hardly have caught one of the neighborhood coyotes and slaughtered it for food, no matter how desperate life could be for someone unhoused.

He'd eaten roadkill raccoon once but swore he'd never do it again.

The blood was only a trickle, and I tried to convince myself Nick had taken up painting with acrylics to while away the hours. Perhaps he'd finally braved his first sip of red wine and gotten so drunk he dropped the bottle. Maybe this was evidence of a bladder infection. A kidney stone. I knocked on the door.

"Nick?" I called out. "You okay? Nick?"

No sound other than the swoosh of a bicycle zooming downhill on the other side of the street. No movement inside the camper.

I repeated the mantra I made myself say out loud at least twice a day. "If you are brave, you are likely to make mistakes. Be brave anyway."

I set my two bags of groceries on the sidewalk and pushed down on the handle. The latch clicked. "Nick?"

I pulled the door open and peered cautiously inside. Nick was sitting on the camper's tiny loveseat, leaning against a narrow closet. An open plastic wrapper on a tiny pull-down table revealed the last two slices of wheat and walnut bread from a loaf I'd bought him the week before. Underneath the table was a black garbage bag filled with trash that I was scheduled to take away today after dropping off Nick's groceries.

I staggered and caught myself on the doorframe, remembering the death oaths I'd made in the Idaho Falls temple years before. We'd all promised upon pain of death never to divulge the secret handshakes needed to get us into heaven. Those of us taking out our endowments agreed to be disemboweled if we revealed the secret. We agreed to have our throats slit.

Nick Degraff had been Mormon.

His throat was slit.

I closed my eyes and swallowed the bile in my mouth. Then I pulled out my cell and dialed 9-1-1.

***

Detective Stalder surveyed me again with a quick flicker of his eyes. He'd done it several times already as we talked outside the camper. "Morgan sounds like a girl's name," he said. It was the third homophobic thing he'd said since he and his partner had arrived.

I thought about Inspector Vivaldi and shrugged. "Stalder sounds like a prick's name." When the detective scowled, I added casually, "So it's plenty butch, I suppose."

Detective Stalder looked unsure if he'd been insulted or not. But if he was too dense to understand, that was on him. He turned to his partner, Detective Klimczyk. "Seems Mr. Degraff brought the wrong guy home for sex."

Detective Klimczyk looked on impassively.

"Nick wasn't gay," I said. The detective was making assumptions about Nick based on my own appearance and manner, as if gay and straight men could never be friends. And did he not think women capable of murder? Didn't he watch *Law and Order*?

Detective Stalder looked me up and down yet again. "Uh huh."

"You seem to have exceptionally strong gaydar for a straight man," I said in as neutral a tone as I could muster. It was difficult not to hear disdain in his voice, even if intellectually I realized I might be imagining it. Years ago, one of my fuck buddies had been stabbed to death by a gay basher, and the responding officers had basically determined Kevin got what he deserved. Before I came out, I remembered my bishop announcing the excommunication of a young man in the Elders Quorum.

"He's dying of AIDS," Bishop Hauer had added. "Let's all pray he repents while he has time. But if he chooses spiritual death the way he chose physical death, so be it."

"Listen, you—"

"You already told us Mr. Degraff was getting a messy divorce," Detective Klimczyk interrupted. "How do you know he wasn't gay? People have secrets." He raised an eyebrow. "No offense, Mr. Beylerian, but just because he wasn't interested in *you* doesn't mean he wasn't gay."

Both detectives were about forty, white, and in good enough shape that I'd have happily knelt for them under other circumstances, but obnoxiousness was a real turn off for pretty much any body type.

To be fair, it was mostly Stalder who was obnoxious, though it was difficult to see the other detective as his own person since they worked as a team. Klimczyk did have sexy ears, though, so I wanted to give him the benefit of the doubt.

The kind of ears you wanted to slowly caress with your tongue and…

"*You* could probably turn a gay man straight." Detective Stalder smirked, pointing a stubby finger at my belly.

"Are these the investigative techniques they're teaching these days?" I shot back. "I might be fat, but I'm good. Nick had me give him blow jobs all the time. He had no reason to lie about his orientation."

"I'll pass," Stalder said.

"I wasn't offering."

"Mr. Beylerian," Klimczyk interjected softly, "we'll investigate every possibility, including whether or not this was a sex crime."

The truth was I had no idea if Nick's murder was sex-related or not. I couldn't think of any reason at all someone would want to kill him. I *liked* the guy. We played backgammon together. We chatted while playing gin rummy. If I hadn't liked him, there were plenty of other homeless folks I could have helped instead. There was certainly no shortage.

Nick still resisted granting a temple divorce to Amanda despite having already agreed to a civil one, but it was hard to imagine she'd have killed him over it. Or hired someone else to do it. Nick and I joked that instead of being a Stepford Wife, Amanda was a Schroedinger's Wife, married and not married to him at the same time. But then Nick's smile would fade and he'd say, "As long as our marriage survives on any plane, there's still hope it's not dead."

"Did you ever see him with anyone else?" Klimczyk asked.

I shrugged. "I probably only spent two or three hours a week with him," I said. "That leaves…what?…a hundred and sixty-something hours I can't claim to have witnessed."

But it wasn't as if anyone was fighting him over his parking spot alongside Takahashi Gardens. There was nothing besides trees and bushes along this stretch of Renton Avenue. And it was far enough uphill that no one casually walked by who wasn't headed this way with a firm destination in mind.

It wasn't Rainier and Henderson, where I'd once dodged bullets from a drive-by shooting, or where I'd witnessed two teenage girls mug an old man about my age.

Another day at that same intersection, I'd seen a patrol car in the bank's parking lot, two officers watching as a young black woman in flashy hooker clothes waited on the corner. Two black men in a faded gray pickup truck pulled into the lot and honked. The young woman had walked over and climbed in between them. The patrol car didn't move as the truck drove off.

Part of me had been glad the officers didn't harass the woman. But another part of me had worried, wondering if she would make it home safely.

"Think he was paying runaways?" Stalder asked. "Street hustlers?"

"Insecure straight men leading a murder investigation," I said. This wasn't Capitol Hill, after all, or Pioneer Square. "You guys think about dick even more than gay men do."

Stalder took a half step forward. Klimczyk put a hand on his arm.

"Me thinketh the detective doth obsess too much," I said.

I didn't even know why I was antagonizing them. It was only going to make life harder for all of us. And it wasn't going to help Nick any.

He needed help, even if he was dead.

Nick's ex had been turning their kids against him. It was almost all we talked about, strategies for winning back their love despite the lies Amanda was telling them.

I was the only other person besides Amanda he'd ever had sex with. And he had been the one to proposition me. He needed some way to deal with both his stress and anger, and he said that if he limited his "release" to a single person he wasn't attracted to, he could convince himself he was only transgressing and not sinning.

A Mormon distinction.

In addition to grocery shopping, sex was one of the few other volunteer activities I participated in. A firefighter here. A police officer there. A straight neighbor whose wife with dementia had been moved into an assisted living facility. And a couple of homeless men.

Lots of folks had limited options but everyone deserved at least the opportunity for sex. It was a principle I believed in as strongly as mail-in voting. As a result, apparently, I gave off "whatever you need, dude" vibes. God only knew how. I embarrassed myself every time I looked in a mirror. So it was almost always other guys doing the asking. Most of the men didn't even seem gay. I assumed it was impolite to ask, the way prisoners never asked each other why they were doing time. Now that I was in the bariatric program and losing weight in preparation for surgery, guys had stopped asking only for blow jobs. Some now wanted to fuck me, too.

It was hardly a sacrifice on my part. I had plenty of my own frustration and anger to deal with. I could often hear Tony beating off in the bathroom right before bed, loud on purpose to warn me not to get frisky later.

Last week, just as I heard him approaching climax, I broke into the chorus of "Suddenly Seymour" right outside the bathroom door.

"Doesn't matter," Stalder said, shrugging. "If he let you into his camper, he could have—"

"He was afraid," I said.

"Of?" asked Klimczyk.

"Everyone."

A few weeks back, a Filipino teenager had been shot several blocks over while opening his front door. A month earlier, a white high school football player had been shot in his car in front of his house. And a retired black nun had been murdered in her home a year ago by a homeless man she volunteered with.

"Except you?" Stalder said with a smile. "You realize you're making yourself the most likely suspect."

I shook my head. "I'm an ex-Mormon," I said. "I'd never be a Danite."

"What the fuck—"

"Look it up."

***

Before walking the last few blocks home, I handed the two bags of groceries to Elijah, Nick's closest homeless neighbor. I suppose homeless wasn't the best word. Unhoused, either. Several folks along this stretch of Renton Avenue lived in campers, vans, RVs, and long-haul trucker cabs. They all technically had roofs over their heads, just extremely inadequate ones.

I was too lazy and self-centered to do any real advocacy work, but I did try to pick up trash bags from several of the homeless folks along Renton. Made me feel more useful than I really was, and it did reduce illegal dumping in the gully beside Takahashi Gardens.

Mr. Takahashi had run a nursery in Rainier Beach early in the twentieth century. He and his family had been interned in a concentration camp during WWII, but after the war, he still ended up donating his property to the City of Seattle, and they eventually turned it into a Japanese garden.

"Morgan," Tony said as I walked in the door, "what took you so long? Dinner's been ready for ages."

"Sorry, sweetie." I kissed my husband and then wrapped my arms around him and didn't let go.

"Is something wrong?" Tony asked. "What happened?"

"Nick was murdered in his camper."

"Jesus, Morgan, you need to stop hanging out with dangerous people."

I took a step back. "You used to take out the nun's trash, didn't you?"

"That was different. *She* wasn't dangerous."

"Elijah doesn't seem dangerous. I'll start visiting him now."

"Jesus, Morgan."

Nick had given me a silver Morgan dollar last week, said it had been given to him by his grandfather, who'd claimed that *his* father had received it from Lorenzo Snow.

People sometimes gave away their prized possessions before taking their own lives.

Had Nick *asked* someone to kill him? Provoked someone?

"I'm going to wash my face."

"Hope you're in the mood for chili."

I nodded and continued to the bathroom. The sad truth was that I was in fact hungry. I was always hungry. Drinking lots of water didn't help. Using little spoons and forks didn't help. Keeping a food diary didn't help.

It simply added to the mortification.

I didn't blame Tony for not understanding that beans had too many carbs for me. It seemed unfair for the bariatric clinic to force me to lose twenty pounds on my own as one of a dozen hoops I had to jump through to qualify for surgery. If I could lose that much weight by myself, I wouldn't need to cut two-thirds of my stomach off.

Still, unexpected gum surgery in early August had forced me onto a liquid diet for a week, during which I'd lost an amazing fifteen pounds, so I'd kept it up for an additional week and lost six more. I'd gone from 244 pounds—the lowest weight at which I qualified for the program—down to 219. But it was a constant battle not to regain even a pound. If I did, I could still get kicked out of the program.

Tony had weighed 160 when we first met seventeen years ago. He weighed 164 now.

"You don't like it?" Tony asked after I joined him at the table without picking up my spoon. He frowned. "I tried not to make it too spicy."

"I'm sure it's great," I said. "I'm just not very hungry after seeing Nick with his throat slit." He'd interpret any other explanation as a personal attack.

"Jesus, Morgan. I'm eating."

I shrugged. "I need to take advantage of every inspiration not to eat."

Tony rolled his eyes. "Fine. Keep hanging out with dangerous people. Maybe you'll be shot in the stomach and the doctor will be forced to do the bypass sooner."

He wasn't really being mean, I kept telling myself. Not intentionally, anyway. He just had an odd sense of humor that seemed to tickle his own funny bone more than anyone else's.

"How much money do you think a homeless man keeps in his camper?" I asked.

"Huh?"

"Why do you suppose he was killed?"

Tony shook his head, clearly unhappy with the topic. "Maybe it was just someone killing random homeless people. Like that serial killer in Stockton. Or the guy who set that homeless man on fire in Chicago. These things happen all the time." He shrugged.

I took another sip of seltzer water. Lime was my favorite, and Tony always remembered to buy it. Technically, I wasn't supposed to drink anything carbonated once I was in the bariatric program because it irritated the stomach lining. But I needed something with "body." I was sure I could stop before having my endoscopy and again when it came time for the actual surgery. There weren't any twelve-step programs for seltzer water, after all.

I was already able to stand up from the sofa now using only my legs, without needing to push up with my arms at the same time.

The liquid diet had forced me to take in only 20 to 30 grams of carbs a day. I'd been able to eliminate insulin injections completely for six weeks. Once I was back on solid food, though, even trying to keep my carbs low, I couldn't keep them low enough. I'd eventually had to start injecting again once a day, and within another two weeks was injecting twice a day as I'd been doing for years.

One of the side effects of insulin was weight gain.

It was also one of the side effects of my HIV meds.

"A pedestrian was killed in a hit-and-run on Capitol Hill," Tony said, taking advantage of my silence to shift the conversation.

"Anyone we know?"

He shook his head.

"That's three pedestrians hit by cars in the past two weeks," I noted. All hit-and-run. Was this the work of a serial killer, too?

"And a home invasion in Ballard."

I picked some cheese off the top of my chili and ate it. "I suppose it's still a home invasion if your home is a camper, isn't it?"

And it would still be a home invasion if someone broke into your tent. Or accosted you in your sleeping bag.

Tony put his spoon down. "You're killing me with all this homeless talk." He stuck a finger in his chili and pulled it out, orange now from the sauce and spices. He rubbed it on the ridges of his left ear.

I stood up and moved to the other side of the table, leaning down and licking every drop of chili sauce off him.

"You don't like the beans," he said, "but you'll still eat a full protein, right?" He swung his legs away from the table, unzipped, and closed his eyes.

I was up for almost anything that kept me away from the fridge.

Chapter Two: Blood Down the Aisle

"'We don't need gun control,'" I quoted for Tony as I poured his coffee the following morning, "'We need demon control.'" Some right-wing nutjob had said this on national TV.

"No news!" Tony hissed. "I told you not to tell me any news in the morning!"

"Not even about North Korea firing a missile over Japan?"

"Stop it!"

I supposed my sense of humor could be a bit annoying, too, especially in the mornings. None of that was funny. My teasing seemed as passive aggressive as his.

Like the time I'd given Tony a box set of Doris Day's romantic comedies for his birthday even though I was the only one who liked them.

"Can I sing 'For All We Know'?" I started humming.

"Is that a Karen Carpenter song?"

"It won an Oscar."

"Really?"

I began singing.

"Okay, okay. What's the latest on Ukraine?"

I heated some oatmeal for Tony in the microwave and added a dash of milk afterward both for flavor and to cool the mess down a bit. Then I beat an egg, mixed in some Monterey Jack cheese and a spritz of vanilla, and cooked a no-carb chaffle for myself.

Adding butter afterward didn't help my numbers, but I couldn't pour real syrup, and fake syrup was nothing more than flavored laxative.

I hoped Elijah liked the cheese Danish I'd bought for Nick.

Eating in place of another. If Mormonism had taught me anything, it was the value of proxy work.

I'd *enjoyed* watching Nick enjoy himself.

Most days, life seemed little more than total chaos. Somehow, though, Nick's death didn't feel like an isolated data point but part of a larger pattern. Probably the way our minds were wired to see dinosaur shapes in clouds, human faces on Mars, a bunny in the moon.

I didn't update Tony on the latest news about Patti LaBelle being rushed offstage in Milwaukee after a bomb threat. And there was no point talking to him about far-right terrorists threatening to blow up the Children's

Hospital in Boston over gender-affirming care. Or an equally disturbing report about Democrats funding far-right candidates in the hopes that would force voters to choose "sane" Democrats, when using that money to promote useful policies would have been better all around.

Only Democrats didn't really have that many great policies. Biden had included student loan forgiveness as part of his campaign platform, and two years in still hadn't managed to forgive so much as a penny. While broken promises were bad enough, too many other Democrats couldn't be bothered to make promises to begin with.

No universal healthcare. No subsidized childcare. No tuition-free college and vocational training. No fare-free public transit. No housing as a human right.

And no ban on fracking. Even Nick, who was still a registered Republican, had understood that climate breakdown was real.

Tony lusted after Pete Buttigieg, who despite raising two infants of his own couldn't see anything wrong with a system that made it impossible for thousands of parents to find baby formula.

Tony and I didn't talk politics.

High levels of cortisol made people gain weight.

"I know that's not all you're going to eat," Tony said, nodding at the last bite of my chaffle. "You're probably going to buy a donut on your way to work."

"What good would that do?" I asked. "I can't hide carbs or calories from my body. It knows what I take in, whether you or my doctor or anyone else sees it or not."

"I bet you eat *two* donuts every morning," Tony said. "You couldn't eat just this piddly stuff every day and not lose more weight."

"I sure wish you'd put some of that money you earn as a doctor toward the mortgage."

"Fuck you."

"I'm up for a protein suppository." Zero calories.

Tony pointed his finger and imitated the Soup Nazi from *Seinfeld*. "No nookie for you!"

***

The Ethiopian church across the street had installed a black iron fence over the past few weeks, so I couldn't cut across their property any longer to reach the bus stop. That meant walking an extra half block up a steep hill and then walking back downhill another half block. It wasn't as if I didn't need the exercise. I just hated to be panting when the bus pulled up. No one wanted to sit beside a heavy breather, mask or no mask.

Not that most other folks were worried about the pandemic anymore, three years in. As we moved into colder weather, the country was seeing huge spikes in the number of COVID cases, flu, and RSV, in addition to everyday colds.

I didn't want any of them. Whenever someone without a mask sat next to me, I'd nod pleasantly and say, "I'll trade my head lice for your respiratory virus," and then tilt my head in their direction.

The bus was late, but that gave me time to catch my breath. I looked downhill toward Takahashi Gardens.

Nick's wife might not have had anything to do with his murder, but she was probably happy about it regardless. Made her life easier. His kids might care someday, but that day wasn't today. The police had lots of other crimes to solve. Crimes that affected more important people than a homeless guy in a camper.

What if I was the only person who cared that Nick was dead?

The more relevant question was what good was it to "care" if I wasn't going to *do* anything about it?

I watched European detective shows just to hear French and German and Italian, but that didn't qualify me to find Nick's killer.

Perhaps after work, I could stop and talk to Elijah. Maybe call the precinct to get an update.

Of course, even if I hadn't been a total jerk with those detectives, they'd hardly talk to me about a case in which I was probably still a suspect. They'd made me go down to the station near Othello to complete my statement yesterday afternoon, just blocks from where I'd taken part in a Black Lives Matter protest shortly after the pandemic began. The little park where I could legally deposit my sharps containers, a fifteen-minute bus ride away from the house.

I'd had to catch the 106 back to Rainier Beach yesterday after signing my statement. I'd seen Tockner at the station but didn't make eye contact. He was one of the officers I blew every few weeks, gay but closeted. He'd been driving his personal vehicle and pulled over to offer me a lift sometime last January when it snowed and the 106 wouldn't go up the hill. He hadn't noticed I was gay until I climbed into his car. When I asked if there was anything I could do to thank him, well...

I heard the familiar hum of a Metro bus and turned around to see the 106 coming over the top of the hill from Skyway. I swung my bag to catch the driver's attention. Buses sometimes flew past this stop without slowing down.

The driver pulled over to the curb but slightly past me, so that I had to squeeze in by the light pole.

Jerk.

I climbed on, leaned over to tap my badge on the fare reader, and started down the aisle.

"I told you to stop that!" the driver ordered.

I paused, confused. Then I noticed a stream of water down the aisle and tracked it to its source. In the middle of the back seat sat a young black woman with her leggings pulled down below her knees. She had lifted her skirt and was pouring a bottle of water over her privates.

I stood rooted in place. No wonder the driver had overshot.

Nick had refused to ride public transit. He might be homeless, he said, but he hadn't yet sunk that low.

"It's my monthly blood!" the woman shouted back. She had an African accent, though my ignorant ear couldn't pinpoint it any more specifically than that. "I can't walk around all bloody!"

"You don't clean up on the bus!" The driver had an African accent, too.

"Well, I can't wash myself on the street!"

I made my way to a seat two rows behind the Disability section and sat down next to a tiny Asian woman who was pretending not to notice the conversation. Everyone else was doing the same.

"Get off the bus."

"I'm not getting off until I get to my destination." Despite her accent, she spoke quite clearly.

It struck me that as outrageous as her behavior was, it alone probably qualified her for U.S. citizenship, if she wasn't already naturalized. One right-wing pundit, after all, was claiming that men having sex with women was "gay." Another suggested that the recent shooting of an elementary school teacher by a six-year-old student wouldn't have happened if we simply armed our teachers and she could have shot first.

And in the latest political ad from a white, blonde Republican troll, the woman boarded a helicopter and aimed an assault weapon at feral hogs on the ground below, comparing them to Democrats, who she labeled Communists. "Save America!" a banner on the TV proclaimed as she opened fire.

The driver closed the doors and drove on. More water trickled down the aisle. I noticed that only three other riders wore masks. One woman had a mask on her chin but kept her nose uncovered so she could keep wiping away mucus with her fingers.

Masks weren't mandated anywhere these days. Why bother fake-wearing a mask if you didn't want to wear one? I understood the scriptural aversion to lukewarm commitment better after riding the bus than I ever did from a talk in Sacrament meeting.

Mormons weren't allowed to discuss outside the temple what they learned inside the temple, yet in the temple, we were either in "class" watching a movie and learning handshakes, or in the prayer circle chanting while pawing at the air like cats, or in the Celestial Room, where no one was allowed to talk at all. So I'd never been able to ask anyone why we pretended to slit our throats and disembowel ourselves. After being excommunicated, I no longer cared.

What thoughts had gone through Nick's mind when that knife sliced across his throat?

I closed my eyes. No matter how awful it must be to die alone, how much more awful must it be to die *not* alone, in the company of someone who wanted you dead?

Was there anyone to hug Nick on the Other Side?

Was there an Other Side at all?

Nick's murder hadn't even made the local news. Instead, there'd been a lengthy report about a gang of thieves ripping ATMs out of stores when the businesses were closed overnight.

Several stops later, we were at the corner of Henderson and Rainier. The driver again ordered the woman off the bus. She again refused. When I scanned the vehicle, I could see the other riders still pretending they hadn't noticed a thing. No one was even grumbling under their breath, at either the driver or the bathing woman.

I thought about Bathsheba.

Instead of getting off the bus, the woman grabbed several masks from the dispenser and threw them on the floor, using her foot to wipe up the liquid. When the driver asked what she was doing, she told him, "I accidentally spilled some water while I was cleaning myself."

"It wasn't an accident," the driver said. "You poured that water on purpose."

I remembered the initiatory in the temple, when an old man had reached underneath the sheet I was wearing to wash me and then anoint me with oil.

"What do you mean? Why are you saying that? You're hurting my feelings!"

"Get off the bus or I'll call the police."

"Fine! I'm not getting off the bus!"

"I can wait."

"You want to play that game? I can wait, too!"

With all the craziness in the world, with a growing pandemic of Karens, with road rage its own crime category, perhaps it was inevitable that another person I knew had been murdered.

I'd watched *22 July* on my last day off, without Tony, who didn't like political movies. It showed the horrors committed by a white nationalist who'd killed 77 people in Norway to protest immigration. One of the main characters, a teen who'd been shot five times, was from Svalbard.

That was the starting point for The Arctic Circle expedition I'd applied for, a two-week stint on a sailing vessel. If I was selected in February, I'd fly to Norway next October. I'd use the experience to write an op-ed about climate breakdown.

Because my incredible op-ed, obviously, would change the world.

While I recklessly used tons of resources for the opportunity to "help" others.

Outrageous.

The woman continued wiping the aisle with COVID masks, the driver not saying another word. He had not raised his voice even during this interaction, though the woman certainly did. When she reached my row to mop, huffing and puffing without a mask, she put her hand on the back of the seat in front of me. Her nails were long and painted different colors, with glitter on some of them.

I wasn't *terribly* observant, but *maybe* if I returned to Nick's camper, I'd notice something the detectives hadn't.

A passenger behind me finally did mutter a complaint to the driver, who couldn't possibly hear him from that distance, "At least close the doors. It's cold." It may have been sixty degrees.

Seattleites wore parkas during our mild winters, and parkas with shorts in the summer.

Nick still wore his Mormon underwear, even when I was sucking him off.

The woman dragging her foot down the aisle thought the passenger was addressing her and asked sharply, "What did you say!?"

The man shook his head. "Nothing."

No one else said a word as the woman continued to wipe dirty water across the floor of the bus and complain and complain. Finally, after ten minutes, she said, "Okay. I'll get off. Should I leave by the front door or the back door?"

The driver didn't answer. Both doors were open so she could leave without the driver ever needing to say another word.

"I can't leave unless you tell me what door to leave from! What door? Should I leave by the front door or the back door?"

The driver remained silent. No other passengers said a word. As the only white passenger, I wasn't about to say anything. None of us wanted to do anything at all that might escalate the situation.

Finally, the woman kicked several dirty masks out the back door onto the parking strip and stepped off. The driver closed the door and drove on. And still no one said a word.

It was 8:16 a.m. Giving up caffeine was a requirement for the bariatric program. That was proving to be far more difficult than giving up carbs.

Chapter Three: Blood from a Stone

"Hi, Morgan!" my coworker called out as I walked into the bank five minutes late after all the watery drama on the bus.

"Hey, Mirelle."

"Jeez, you look like shit."

A previous husband, now deceased, had gifted me with some fossilized dinosaur dung for Christmas, so it wasn't the most disturbing comment I'd heard so far today. "Love your earrings." My coworker was wearing pewter fruit flies. They'd look great next to the coprolite specimen.

"You know I buy these things just for you," Mirelle told me.

"Your boyfriend doesn't notice them?"

"He didn't even notice my new tattoo."

"Was it somewhere he'd normally look?"

Mirelle paused. "Well, usually the lights are off by that point."

"Keep it professional, guys." That was Joshua, our manager.

Mirelle was another bank teller, in her early twenties, her hair a different color every few weeks. Today, it was purple on one side and blue on the other. Her skin was practically alabaster, making any color she chose striking. She painted a beauty mark on a different part of her face each time she changed her hair.

Joshua was only a few years older, perhaps thirty or thirty-one. He was white as well, though his skin wasn't quite as incandescent.

Jevin was down at the last window, a slim white twink.

After I logged onto my station and counted my drawer, I sent a quick email to Metro commending my driver for professionally handling the ablutions that morning.

"Do anything fun last night?" Mirelle asked from her station next to mine. We'd long had bullet-proof glass to separate us from the customers, but during the pandemic, management had added plexiglass partitions between the tellers as well. Unfortunately, there was a gap of about six inches so that the new partitions between the computers didn't reach the ones facing the customers. I'd tried various ways to block the gaps on either side of my station to reduce viral particles drifting my way from coworkers, but Joshua deemed every attempt "unprofessional" and ordered me to take them down.

He'd finally allowed a long, single strip of light green acrylic attached with double stick tape. I'd convinced him the green showed "team spirit" for customers who were residents of the Emerald City. The bank wouldn't fork out any money for the strips, but Joshua allowed me to use my own funds and then set up the strips myself at each of the six teller stations one afternoon after we closed.

That left the little mouth hole at face level in the front partition. Customers routinely pulled down their masks, assuming they were wearing them at all, and put their mouths up to the hole to conduct their transaction.

I'd tried taping a sticky note advertising car loan rates over the opening, and after Joshua vetoed that, I tried fastening a plastic page protector over it, but Joshua ordered that down as well, so I usually waited to cover the hole until he was in a meeting or if a customer with problematic sinus issues walked up and I simply had no choice but to defy orders.

"I found a dead body."

Mirelle laughed a moment and then frowned. "Oh, wait," she said. "You're serious?"

I explained what happened, but before she could say much more, it was time to open. At least Joshua didn't insist we come in early for a morning pep rally. Those reminded me too much of morning devotionals during my mission to Italy.

"Quanti simpatizzanti troverete oggi?"

I always swore to find as many new investigators as the district leader did. It wasn't difficult to achieve, as almost none of us ever taught more than a couple of lessons in an entire week.

My morning at the teller window passed uneventfully. I deposited or cashed checks, made loan payments, transferred funds, almost all things that could be done by customers themselves at an ATM or at home on the computer. Older folks used Paypal. Younger folks deposited occasional checks using their cell phones. Many people simply transferred funds with Venmo or Cash App.

I'd never asked Nick to pay anything toward the food I brought him, and after that first visit, he could request the specific foods he wanted, not simply accept what I deigned to purchase. It was my limited version of GiveDirectly or Universal Basic Income. Nick hadn't moved the camper once since I first noticed it and so didn't need to refuel often. I assumed he had money somewhere, even if not much, but I'd never asked where he did his banking.

It would be inappropriate to use the bank's computer to look up anyone's personal information.

During a lull just before noon, Joshua walked up to the window from the lobby side of the partition. He was tall and stood on tip toe to speak over the top. "You need to get some credit card referrals," he reminded me. "Interest rates are up."

Predation as customer service.

"Sure thing," I said.

Since our annual bonuses were tied to our success reaching the monthly goals, and the goals were raised every time we reached them, predation was also Joshua's management style.

I couldn't listen to the lyrics for "Sal Tlay Ka Siti" with Tony in the room because I always teared up, and he'd laugh.

Mirelle went on her lunch first, so Jevin was the only other teller on duty with me, three windows down. He was even younger than Mirelle and looked at his phone whenever no one was in line.

Which meant he rarely noticed when the next person walked up to the "Wait to be called" sign. "Over here." I waved to a guy around forty. He nodded and headed to my window. "Wow," I said when I got a closer look. "Love your ammonites." His earrings were brown, fossilized shells with a touch of gold, each affixed to a large-gauge piercing.

"You're the first person who even knows what they are," he said with a laugh.

That seemed unlikely. "They're beautiful."

"Thank you."

I worried the man might think I was coming on to him. He was heavily tatted, but who wasn't these days? His hair was tied in a ponytail, which struck me as a straight man's fashion, and his beard was a little scruffy, though that could simply put him in the leather crowd.

Or the lumberjack crowd.

Damn, but I wanted to stick my tongue through his ear holes.

They were just a bit too small to try inserting anything else.

I counted out his withdrawal carefully, trying not to look like an idiot by handing him the wrong amount after being so fixated. Working at the teller window would be easier once winter arrived and more guys wore hats.

"You live in Rainier Beach, don't you?" the man asked. His ID told me he was Frank Lubenow.

I looked back up at him. "Um…yes?"

"I saw you talking to the police yesterday. What happened?"

"A homeless guy I bring food to was murdered."

"Oh, fuck! I didn't hear anything about a murder!"

"Do you know any of the folks along that stretch?" Perhaps he passed by regularly.

He shook his head, and that seemed to be the end of the discussion. But just as he was putting his wallet back in his pocket, he said, "You bring folks food, huh?"

"Yeah."

"That sounds like something I could do, but…" He sighed and looked nervously toward the door.

"Would you like to come with me a couple of times to see if it feels comfortable?"

"You'd be okay with me tagging along?" His eyes were hazel, green with flecks of gold.

Did straight lumberjacks coordinate their jewelry with their eye color?

I shrugged. "Only if you wear those earrings. Homeless folks need to see pretty things once in a while, too."

I kept a photo album of all my partners and most of my fuck buddies of the past few decades. Everyone was clothed in the photos, of course. I just liked to see their friendly faces and remember their warmth. I had a separate album for platonic friends and liked to flip through those pages, too.

I hadn't added many photos to either album over the past few years. Tockner wouldn't let me take a picture and I didn't feel particularly close to anyone else I'd met since the pandemic began, but Nick had allowed me to snap a photo not quite a week ago.

I'd looked at his face again last night, like that of the selfie a smiling buddy had sent me half an hour before the first waves hit the beach in Khao Lak.

The actress playing Marlene from *Criminal Games* had barely survived. I could almost make myself believe Joey was alive again every time I saw her onscreen.

Lumberjack Frank chuckled and jotted down his number on a blank deposit slip before leaving.

"We're out of paper," Jevin said a moment later, looking over at me from his station.

I watched Frank walk out the front door and then went to the supply closet to grab another ream so I could load it into the printer.

An older woman—well, my age—had gone up to Jevin's window and tapped on it, so no one else was waiting in line for the time being. Maybe...

Nicholas Degraff. A checking account with $913.58. And a savings account with $40.

No other accounts, though there might be some closed ones on another screen. But I'd snooped more than I should have already.

With his savings account under $300, he was being debited $25 a month from his checking as a penalty.

Did I dare look up recent transactions?

Oh my god.

Going back three months, Nick had not deposited any funds whatsoever. Other than the $25 debited automatically from his checking each month, it looked like he'd made only a single physical withdrawal every four weeks.

He was living on $200 a month.

Well, one $200 withdrawal was from three months ago. I'd started visiting him a month later. The following month, he'd also withdrawn $200, but this past month, he'd only withdrawn $80.

Even losing just $105 a month, Nick had at best a handful of months left before he was penniless. No income at all. When I'd asked if he received SNAP benefits, he'd shaken his head without explaining.

Nick certainly couldn't afford a lawyer. Or alimony.

No need to pay tithing.

But there was a single payment for $5 made just four days ago. To a leukemia research foundation.

I'd told Nick about my mother's death at the age of forty-three just the day before he made that transaction.

He'd never said a word.

"Hel-*lo*!" a middle-aged woman called from the line.

I waved her over. "Good afternoon, ma'am!" I smiled. "How can I help you today?"

Chapter Four: Man in the Torn, Red Slip

Some days, it felt quicker to catch light rail after work and then transfer to the 106 once I was back in Rainier Beach. But today had been the wrong day to gamble. Hordes of attendees for a Comicon boarded one stop before me, heading home after the day's activities. Wizards and space princesses and lizard aliens—the kind of folks some right-wing politicians believed were real.

Who was running the asylum?

At least some of the aliens were wearing masks. From an advanced civilization, apparently.

When we pulled into the Mount Baker light rail station, I casually glanced over at the northbound platform while waiting for folks to board and deboard my southbound train. A tall, burly black man with a beard stood on the yellow warning strip. Over his white tank top, he wore a woman's torn, dirty red slip. He also wore gray socks and too-small tennis shoes he could only fit onto his feet by stepping on the heels and treating the shoes as slippers.

He wore no underwear, which became apparent when he flashed everyone on our train. Before we left, the northbound train pulled up and the man in the red slip boarded.

Nick had been proud he hadn't succumbed to the temptation to drink.

Diseases of despair.

Sometimes, folks made bad choices. But few people took their first drink intending to become alcoholics. By the time they realized they were addicts, it was no longer a simple thing to stop. It was why I still hadn't had so much as a single sip of alcohol all these years after leaving the Mormon faith. I wasn't sure I'd be strong enough to get into rehab or join AA. Better not to take the risk.

It wasn't as if I couldn't still get up on a bar fully sober and dance.

Back in the day.

I was tempted by edibles, though. Did anyone make low-carb pot brownies? Maybe I'd look into it after my surgery.

My latest hurdle had been an appointment with a bariatric psychiatrist, to determine if I was mentally sound enough to handle a drastic lifestyle change. "Have you ever thought about hurting yourself?"

Who in their right mind would admit to such a thing when doing so would prevent you from getting what you needed?

Mental health, like vision and dental, was not part of healthcare. My insurance through the bank allowed three visits per year "per issue." But what issue worth talking about could be resolved in three sessions? And if you were a doctor or police officer or shooting instructor, you didn't want it getting out you needed psychiatric help. So you went without, whether you could afford it or not.

I told the bariatric psychiatrist I felt fine, was in a strong marriage, and had realistic expectations about the surgery.

I pulled out my cell as the train reached Othello and texted Frank to arrange meeting at Safeway after work the next evening. Afterward, I could take the opportunity to ask Elijah and some of the other campers a few questions.

Of course, the case might be solved by then. Murders were usually solved within the first two days if they were ever going to be. Or was that missing persons cases? I paid more attention to the language than to procedure when I watched detective shows.

The most irritating part was always when the main character was having a serious discussion with their child or significant other and then the phone rang and they felt compelled to answer. They'd run out immediately to take care of something that could easily have waited five measly minutes so their discussion could get past that critical moment. They weren't firefighters, after all, or paramedics.

"Could you move your bag?" a voice asked. A woman in her early thirties, dressed in an expensive looking blouse with lots of buttons, had just boarded light rail.

"I can if you put on a mask," I returned.

"I don't have to put on a mask!" she spat. Literally. I felt the spray on my arm.

"No, you don't," I said. "Just as I don't have to move my bag." I looked at her a moment. "We can cooperate or not as you see fit."

"Asshole."

"Do you kiss your dog with that mouth?"

The woman looked about and saw that the only other free seats were next to homeless folks slumped over, with food wrappers on the seat next to them. The space princesses and wizards sat together. The woman grabbed a surgical mask from the dispenser near the door and pulled it on, the mask bunching up above her chin and below her nose, making it look as if she were wearing light blue lipstick.

"Happy now?"

I shook my head. "This isn't about coercion. It's about viral spread."

"Asshole."

"Since you keep bringing it up, I hope you get your kids vaccinated against HPV." It was probably too late for her. Such a widespread virus.

Bird flu was on the rise as well. Buying eggs for my chaffles was getting expensive.

The woman removed her mask and stood next to my row, breathing so heavily I thought she might hyperventilate. A lizard person from across the aisle got up and moved away, but the heavily buttoned woman standing beside me didn't take his place.

One more stop, I thought. I closed my eyes and pretended to sleep, thinking that might encourage her to give up, but of course it didn't. She just breathed even more loudly. So I pulled out my phone and started recording.

"What the hell do you think you're doing!" she demanded.

"Making you famous," I told her.

She finally huffed off, but before she was out of earshot, I called after her, "Love your gingko earrings, by the way!"

I hoped she didn't think I was being sarcastic.

***

"Nick, Nick, Nick," Tony said. "I'm so sick of hearing about Nick."

I thought about Eve Plumb.

Then, for the first time, the briefest of suspicions flashed through my mind. Could *Tony* have killed Nick out of jealousy?

The thought faded away as quickly as it had arisen. Tony was far too petty for something like that. He might have tagged Nick's camper or reported him for illegal camping, but he wouldn't have killed the guy. Too much risk to himself.

"I'm going out for a while." Tony grabbed his wallet. "I'll probably have a sleepover with Ben or Carey."

I nodded. "Have fun."

Tony shrugged. "Whatever I do, it'll be more fun than talking about Nick."

I was itching to talk to Nick's neighbors but was too scared to do it the day after his murder. Somehow, that felt too suspicious. Waiting until tomorrow, though, made me feel I was letting a prisoner escape.

I'd dithered sixty years of my life away.

I looked out the speakeasy window in our front door as Tony hopped onto his e-bike and zipped off down the street.

Tony and I had always had our separate friends and interests. That was one reason our marriage had lasted so long. Seventeen years and counting, far longer than any of my previous relationships. Tony had a better paying job than I did, though, and his e-bike allowed him to visit friends more easily after work and on weekends, on Capitol Hill or in Fremont or in Ballard or wherever.

There was no way I was heading out for Bear Night, leaving the bar at 10:00 and facing a 90-minute commute home after a long day at work.

I knew a friendly leatherman in Columbia City. There was one delivery driver who could cum in thirty seconds who popped his dick in my mouth whenever he was in the neighborhood. And I visited platonic friends, too, a straight couple here in Rainier Beach who had a huge redwood as big around as a Fiat 500 in their front yard. They and their daughter liked to play Scrabble.

And there was always Tockner, the closeted police officer.

The theme music for *Francis, the Talking Mule* drifted through my head.

I walked down Renton and looked across the street at the campers parked alongside Takahashi Gardens, and then I walked back home.

"Hi, Mr. Beylerian," Krichelle said when I called. "To what do we owe the pleasure?"

"This is kind of last minute, but if you and Roger are up to a game of Scrabble, I'd love to invite myself over."

"Hmm."

"Tony just bought a box of Baci for himself that I can confiscate."

"We'll have the board set up by the time you get here. I'll ask Valentina if she wants to join us."

"Sounds great!"

"Give us fifteen minutes so we can test first."

"I'll do the same."

I'd met Roger and Krichelle Duga years ago when caucusing for Bernie Sanders, back when Washington state still held caucuses. The system was terribly flawed, though, so I was glad we'd moved to mail-in ballots for every primary and election. But that caucus system did give me the chance to meet some like-minded neighbors. There weren't many. Sanders had lost in the first round.

I brought the Baci and some Perrier sparkling water that had been on sale at Grocery Outlet.

Did water have an expiration date?

***

"So this Nick guy was murdered?" Krichelle asked. She made the word "star" on the Scrabble board. She and her husband were both in their early forties, both dark haired, though Krichelle kept her hair cropped close so that she could carve the names of famous authors on the back of her scalp throughout the school year. Emily Bronte. Shirley Jackson. Toni Morrison.

I posted an index card on the bookshelf over my computer with my favorite Morrison quote: "I insist on being shocked. I am never going to become immune. I think that's a kind of failure to see so much of it that you die inside. I want to be surprised and shocked every time."

"I'll bet Nick was no saint!" Valentina quipped. Roger gave her a look.

"I Googled his name to see if I could find out what happened at his workplace," I said. "But there must not have been any legal proceedings. I couldn't find anything."

Valentina added the letters B and A in front of her mother's word, tacking on a D at the end.

"Where did he work?" Roger asked. "Maybe you could look up the company itself and find out something."

I put the word "doze" on the board.

"Good job," Krichelle said, though only my E was on a triple letter score.

"I don't even know the name of the company for sure."

Roger added an R at the end of my word, placing the letters B-U-L-L in front. On a double word score.

"Look up anything that sounds remotely like it," Valentina suggested, "and go down there in person."

I wasn't sure how that would be better than online research. No one was going to volunteer information about a scandal.

Krichelle added an S to "tin," a word Valentina had put on the board a few turns ago.

Valentina didn't even wait two seconds before adding an E and an L.

It helped having a high school teacher for a mother, I supposed. Krichelle and her fellow teachers had gone on strike at the beginning of the school year, demanding a cost-of-living increase. Inflation over the past two years had reached 16% in Seattle. The schools were cutting funds for special needs students. There were a whole host of other issues, but since I didn't have kids, I hadn't paid as much attention as I could have. Still, I did join Krichelle on the picket line on my day off. Once.

"I suppose I could go to his congregation and see what I can find out there." Nick's family had attended a ward up in north Seattle. It was why he'd specifically set up his camper in south Seattle.

I added a P to the front of somebody's "lease."

"You think they'll talk to you?" Valentina asked.

Mormons were nothing if not gossipy, but it was true they usually only gossiped amongst themselves. I remembered a Road Show when I was a kid, the Laurels performing a song from *Hee Haw*. "Oh, you'll never hear me repeating gossip, so you better be sure and listen close the first time!"

My mother had been First Counselor in our ward's Relief Society but had stopped attending after hearing the other ward leaders gossiping under the guise of "helping struggling members." I'd remained active longer than she had.

"You don't think someone at his church killed him, do you?" Roger asked. He made the word "twine" on the board by adding an E to an existing word.

Mormons could be embarrassed enough by the behavior of "bad" members that they'd cut them out of their lives, but they weren't as extreme as Scientologists who considered apostates "fair game." And even they didn't resort to murder as far as anyone knew.

"Oh my god." Krichelle put her hand on her chest.

"What?"

"I'm never this lucky." She put the letters I-N-T-E-R in front of Roger's "twine." On a double word score. "And now I'm in the lead!" she crowed.

"I couldn't have a mother who teaches math," Valentina grumbled. "She has to teach English." Valentina added an S and a W in front of someone's "ill."

Krichelle seemed to be succeeding quite well as a mother and a teacher, I thought. "I don't know that talking to anyone at his work or his church will make a difference," I said. "I just don't want to let any of those folks forget him too soon." I couldn't really *will* his life to have meaning, though, could I? "Even if none of them had anything to do with his murder, they all had something to do with his misery."

The detectives had probably talked to people at both locations already, but it wouldn't hurt to remind his former friends and coworkers that this wasn't over yet.

I put the word "lock" on the board. We were running out of space to make good words.

Yet Roger found a way, adding W-A-R in front of it.

"I hate you," I said.

"Well, I love you," Roger returned, leaning over and kissing me on the cheek. Valentina giggled and grabbed another Baci.

Chapter Five: Man in the Crotchless, Black Jeans

Whoo hoo! I was down to 217 pounds! Only sixty-five more to go.

Nope. I had to make my goal 215 pounds and *then* make a new goal. Just two pounds. That's all I had to worry about.

Dill pickles had no calories, but you could only eat just so many dill pickles. Pickled okra was fun, but it was expensive. I often bought celery and onions and chopped up enough in one sitting to add to meals throughout the week, maybe some bok choy, too, but I was never going to be a competent, creative cook.

And once I started eating peanuts, well, I couldn't stop until I'd taken in two days' worth of protein and three days' worth of fat.

Sometimes, I almost *wanted* to catch COVID so I could lose my sense of taste and smell.

But long COVID was real, and it happened a lot to people my age. And weight.

I'd watched a video this morning showing several women jerking about spastically, claiming it was a reaction to their COVID booster. No physician wanted to outright call them fakers, so they'd simply say, "We haven't seen any documented side effects of that nature."

But already there were parody videos, a young black woman shaking her butt vigorously. "I just got my booster and now I can't stop twerking!" A busty white woman jiggling her tits. "I just got my booster and now I'm making extra cash at a strip club!"

Of course, every medication had consequences, just as avoiding medication had consequences. You took your chances either way, but your chances of suffering with COVID while unvaccinated were worse than suffering complications from a vaccination.

There was still no HIV vaccine after all these years.

Nick had insisted on giving me a priesthood blessing. He hadn't been excommunicated yet, he said, and Heavenly Father knew he was innocent, so he hoped the blessing would still work, even without a second priesthood holder present.

I kissed Tony goodbye after breakfast and headed out the door. He liked to be fucked in the morning, but until my stomach retreated enough for my dick to reach his asshole, that activity was no longer an option. I realized a lot of the bitchy things Tony said to me came out because of his frustration. Even access to casual sex didn't stop a guy from wanting a good sexual relationship with his husband.

Two pounds. Just two pounds.

I transferred buses at the Mount Baker Transit Center, right next to a rival bank. If I worked there, my commute would already be over. But I'd interviewed once before, and they didn't want me.

Several teens chatted near the bus shelter, all of them maskless, two of them coughing. An old, Asian woman, masked, stood near the trash can. A Latino in a dirty hoodie sat sleeping hunched over on the bench. A ruler and three carpenter's pencils jutted out of his pocket. His black jeans had a hole in the crotch so he could reach through and scratch in his sleep.

Of course, my dick *could* have reached Tony's asshole if he'd been more cooperative. I couldn't actually see his hole and so just tried to aim for the right spot. Tony would lie there, bored, saying, "Nope. You're cold. Warmer. Nope, cold again." But he'd make no effort to guide my dick to the right spot. For him, finding his asshole on my own was a test of my worthiness, like pulling a sword out of a stone.

I'd never been any good at blind man's bluff.

The next bus was already crowded when I boarded, but I spotted an empty seat next to the window halfway back, blocked by a thirty-something black man frowning as hard as he could. He ignored me when I paused at his row, so I tapped on his shoulder.

He glared without budging.

"You can let me sit by the window," I said calmly, "you can move over and let me sit by the aisle, or I can sit in your lap. Totally your call."

Standing was a problem mostly because I blocked the aisle and no one could squeeze past me to reach the door.

As it turned out, I got the entire row to myself after the man jumped up and pushed the button near the rear exit. For some reason, no one else wanted to sit next to me, either.

Mirelle wore her gargoyle earrings today. If I wasn't such a wuss, I'd buy a pair of those myself. Except for my trim beard, I could still pass as a Mormon. At least I was wearing my polo shirt with the dinosaur patch on the pocket. Edgy.

I reviewed my note cards after counting my drawer. I'd memorized basic greetings in Romanian, Czech, and Finnish since we served such a diverse clientele, but I couldn't hold conversations in any of those languages. I could barely tell Ukrainian and Russian apart, though, so I didn't even guess anymore. Too risky.

The morning passed uneventfully, other than Mr. Easton coming in to withdraw another $40. It wasn't an unreasonable amount, but the man was growing senile and I was afraid he was forgetting he already had cash on hand or, worse, someone at home might be taking advantage of him. A relative? A nurse? A neighbor?

"I saw the Northern Lights yesterday," he said while I pulled a twenty and two tens from my drawer.

"Really?" There'd been no solar storms lately to bring the lights this far south. And it had been cloudy the previous evening.

"Sally and I watch them every chance we get."

"Sounds lovely." His wife had been dead over five years.

I jotted down the conversation after he left to have documentation if we ever needed to report elder abuse.

I hated this part of the job. You couldn't stand by and let someone be mistreated, but when was it right to step in?

My morose mood followed me into the break room for lunch. Why hadn't any of Nick's extended family stepped in to help him? Not a single work buddy? There was never any way I could have been enough.

I needed to read more books about triumphant living, watch more uplifting films. It might make me feel less crushed by life. And it might give me a fighting chance to be at least minimally effective in "making a difference."

Over the years, I'd volunteered with two different environmental groups but both headquarters had been difficult to reach and I ended up in both cases feeling I was taking part in a greenwashing campaign.

Bringing food to homeless folks a few blocks from my house was doable.

I sat by the bulletin board in the break room to eat homemade pimiento and cheese. Not low cal, but at least carb free. Store-bought pimiento and cheese added high fructose corn syrup. For absolutely no reason. I should really be skipping lunch altogether and taking a thirty-minute walk during my break.

Be brave, I told myself.

I texted Tony a short message. "Hope you're having a good day."

I nodded politely to the loan officers on the other side of the small break room, though they seemed oblivious. Former tellers who'd moved to the platform side, they now felt superior. I mostly ignored them, but then Shanifer said something that caught my ear.

"I was walking my dog last night and almost stepped in a pile of feces."

Gurkirat wrinkled his nose. The loan officers never wore masks even while out in the lobby.

"*Human* feces," Shanifer clarified. "There's litter all over my neighborhood. And needles. It's disgusting. What if my poor Maddie steps on a needle while she's peeing?"

"We should put them all in prison," Gurkirat said. "Or at least in a mental hospital."

A right-wing pundit had recently issued a call to execute homeless people so that American cities could be as clean as the airport in Singapore.

"The City moves them out of the neighborhood," Shanifer agreed, "but they come right back."

I gritted my teeth. Some folks on the City Council had proposed a charter amendment called Compassion Seattle. A deceptive name since it would codify sweeps if passed. Sweeping away trash, when the trash in question was people. Where unhoused folks lost what few belongings they had, including their IDs.

It was difficult to apply for a job without an ID. It was also difficult to qualify for assistance. Or rent an apartment.

City officials deliberately refused to provide trash cans where needed, or they might supply a minimal number but then not assign enough folks to pick up the trash. They refused to provide adequate portable toilets, as if "being tough on human waste" would miraculously eliminate bodily functions. Even the most polite, hygienic person on the planet couldn't cross his legs and clench indefinitely.

"We waste so much money on these losers."

"You're right," I said. "It would be cheaper to house them." I'd written an op-ed about it once, and Krichelle had been kind enough to critique the essay before I sent it off to a California newspaper.

Shanifer and Gurkirat turned in my direction, noticing me for the first time.

"Study after study proves it," I said. I hadn't managed to write any op-eds in months, too tired to do more than jot down a few notes. I'd come up with what I considered a decent quote: "Incremental change is not going to cut it. We either choose radical change...or we'll have cataclysmic change by default."

Only I hadn't decided if I would use the words in a piece about climate, universal healthcare, capitalism, or something else.

I also hadn't decided if it was too pretentious to be effective. Nothing felt right anymore.

My mission president had told us that if the only person we converted during our two years was ourselves, our mission would have been successful.

The loan officers turned away and continued chatting more quietly.

"A friend of mine was homeless," I said, obnoxiously breaking into their conversation again. "He was murdered the other day."

Gurkirat turned to look at me once more. "Well, really, Morgan, what do you expect?"

I stood up, put my mask back on, and walked over to the sink to wash my spoon. "Thanks," I said.

"For what?"

"You guys make me lose my appetite. You're great for my diet. Doctors could prescribe you."

I didn't *mean* to be self-righteous. I cringed listening to myself. And I was only "good" in comparison to people who were absolute jerks. It was a pretty low bar. But how could you go on about your day and pretend nothing was wrong when coworkers said such shitty things?

Ms. Pat, the drug dealer turned comedian, could have retold this story in a way to make everyone laugh.

"There's a reason you're still a teller after all these years," Shanifer said.

Somehow, that didn't feel like the insult she intended it to be.

"It's also why you're going to die poor and alone."

Now *that* was an insult. I nodded and gave her a thumbs up.

She gave me the finger in return.

Chapter Six: Man in the Stained, Blue Sweats

"Ruben used to park his van in front of my house," I told Frank when we met up at Safeway. "He was a friend of a friend and needed a place to stay after his girlfriend kicked him out." I wrestled a shopping cart from a long line that seemed welded together, and we moved into the store.

"How did that go?"

I shrugged. "He brought his own extension cord and plugged it into an outlet on the porch. I was nervous about him coming inside to use the bathroom and shower, but he never even asked. I guess he took care of those things somewhere else."

I steered us to the produce aisle and put a couple of apples into the cart, plus a small bunch of grapes and a few bananas.

"I don't know if I could piss in a bucket."

Pissing would be the least of his worries. There were a couple of "hygiene stations" throughout the city where homeless folks could use the toilet, shower, or do their laundry, and several community centers offered showers as well. Ruben had probably taken care of those tasks at the homes of closer friends.

I pushed the cart to the snack aisle and tossed a couple of jars of peanuts in the basket, along with some chocolate-covered almonds. And a bag of potato chips.

Everyone liked potato chips.

"Did he finally get back on his feet?" Frank asked.

I shook my head. "Tony got tired of him being out front and asked him to leave." He hadn't bothered to discuss it with me ahead of time. "Said Ruben was raising our electric bill."

"Was he?"

I laughed. "I have no idea. But that same day, I came down here for the first time to buy food for some of the other homeless folks in the neighborhood. And I'm sure I spend more now than I did on the extra electricity."

I could win a million dollar lottery and not have enough to help homeless people in just this one city.

Unable to attend a City Council meeting during a discussion on "Taxing the Rich," I'd submitted an online public comment. "If hoarding food is criminal in wartime or famine, why is hoarding money okay during an epidemic of homelessness?" I doubted anyone on the Council even read it.

"What does your husband say about that?"

"Not a word. He only gets upset if I talk about any of the people I meet."

Frank put a hand on my arm, an apology for something someone else he'd never even met had done.

We shopped for just a few more minutes. I threw in four cans of beef and vegetable soup and two packs of vanilla protein shakes. It was impossible to maintain a well-balanced diet if you didn't have access to a refrigerator or a stove.

Beyond that, millions of housed folks in the U.S. lived in food deserts, poor neighborhoods or rural areas with little access to stores that might carry healthy foods even if they did have money.

Transportation deserts, too. One store with great prices was two buses away from our house. Most of the time, I wasn't up to the trip. And King County ran one of the better transit systems.

"What'll you do if the person you're giving this to doesn't like some of the food?"

"There's always another van or camper or RV twenty feet away."

Nick had been a regular guy, with a family, a job, a life. He should matter, I thought, even if he didn't have any of those things now.

"You carry all this by hand?" Frank asked as we checked out.

"On my days off, I bring my personal grocery cart. If I'm doing it after work, I buy what I can carry on the bus. I *don't* walk up the hill."

"Your husband can't drive you?"

"He only has an e-bike." And I couldn't afford to buy more food anyway.

"Well, we've got my car today."

This time, I was the one who put my hand on his arm. "Thank you," I said.

"I hope you know I'm not gay."

It was hard not to laugh, but he was a new ally, and I didn't want to offend him. "I'll have to content myself with fantasizing about your extinct earrings."

Frank grinned and pulled my hand up to touch his ammonites. "Let's go visit the campers."

***

"You need a lift home?" Frank asked after Elijah shut his camper door.

"Thanks. I'll walk the rest of the way." I patted my stomach. "I need to burn off at least another fifteen calories."

Frank chuckled. "Can I come with you another time before I try any of this on my own? I'll foot the bill."

I nodded. Smiling wasn't effective body language when you were masking. "Sounds great."

After Frank drove off, I turned back toward Nick's camper. There was still yellow crime scene tape across the door. I was a bit surprised the vehicle hadn't already been towed and understood it might very well be first thing in the morning.

Nick had worried his camper would be impounded one day while he was out buying food. It had never occurred to me before that the City might essentially steal even these minimal shelters. It cost $1200 to retrieve an impounded vehicle.

If I was going to do any illegal snooping, it would need to be now.

I never stole so much as an ink pen from work.

I was ten before I realized there was no Tooth Fairy, thirteen before I learned the truth about Santa.

I used to phone the radio station request line to ask for the Carpenters' "Calling Occupants of Interplanetary Craft," hoping an alien civilization was monitoring our airwaves.

I stared at the camper door and took a breath. The only real crime I committed these days was jaywalking. When Metro put a bus stop in the middle of the block across the street from the grocery, no one carrying two heavy bags was going to walk all the way to the corner and back, especially when that delay could mean missing the bus and adding another fifteen or twenty minutes to the trip home.

I'd been voted Most Courteous in high school and Most Likely Not to Cheat on His Taxes.

Our class had a lot of superlatives. My girlfriend had been voted Most Likely to Outshine Her Husband.

I studied the light poles closest to Nick's camper for a moment, and a sign warning drivers of a speed bump. I surveyed the branches in some of the nearby trees. I couldn't detect any surveillance cameras, but I expected the police could conceal them if they tried.

I supposed it wouldn't be the end of the world if I was arrested and got a record. If I was any kind of climate activist at all, I'd have been arrested already.

Sucking and fucking had both been felonies when I spent a Mardi Gras in New Orleans years ago, crimes in several other states as well. Pissing into another man's mouth in a French Quarter bathhouse was probably only a misdemeanor.

My first time with a weterosexual.

What if the police were waiting to see if the murderer came back to the scene of the crime? That could even be why the camper hadn't been towed yet. If I wasn't much of a suspect before, I sure would be once I broke that crime scene tape.

For all I knew, the murder had already been solved. It wasn't as if the police were obligated to inform me, as if the news was obligated to report it.

I pulled my keychain from my pocket and sawed at the tape. As a missionary, my keychain had held a vial of consecrated oil so I'd be ready to perform a priesthood blessing in an emergency. Now it held a small pocketknife.

I'd been Nick's emergency.

No one could see me from the street and there were no houses on this side of the camper, just the fence around Takahashi Gardens and lots of vegetation. The camper door wasn't even locked.

A trap?

Peering inside, I knew I was making a fool of myself. Only once in two years had an Italian mistaken me for a fellow native, but there was no way I could pass as a detective. I didn't have the stomach for it.

The blood stains looked black as the sun started setting behind Beacon Hill. The mild disarray showed that Stalder and Klimczyk had thoroughly searched the cabinet and closet. I didn't know what I expected to find that they hadn't.

I opened a cupboard. It held two thick, plastic plates and a pack of paper plates. A single "glass" made of hard plastic and several flimsy plastic picnic cups.

You spent more when you didn't have easy access to running water.

Nick told me he'd grown up in Idaho, as I had, though he'd been much farther north in Coeur d'Alene, where white supremacists had recently showed up in riot gear on Gay Pride Day. Nick had enjoyed cross country skiing as a teen. Did his two-year mission in Puerto Rico. He followed the Knicks just for their name. He met Amanda while adopting an abandoned Malamute at the animal shelter where she volunteered.

Earlier this year, after Nick had been fired for the scandal at work, Amanda had believed him guilty of whatever impropriety he was accused of and that had broken his will to fight. Perhaps trouble had been simmering in the relationship already and his wife had jumped at the chance to justify leaving.

People should be able to leave simply because they wanted to. When my mom had been diagnosed, her first words were, "And things had finally started going well with your dad."

I'd had no idea they hadn't always been going well.

Sometimes, in the evening before bed, I watched music videos online and fantasized about going back in time to show them to my mother. She'd have loved Christina Perri's "Arms" or Pink's "Walk Me Home." I imagined her drooling over Francesco Gabbani singing "Spazio Tempo," as charmed with his smile as I was.

I wanted to be the one to introduce her to the marvels of *Jurassic Park* and *Everything Everywhere All at Once*.

I wanted Nick to watch me solve his murder and know that I missed him even if Amanda didn't.

I opened the tiny closet. One pair of jeans, a single button-down shirt, a Knicks jacket, and three T-shirts. One of them read "Families Are Forever."

It had been a gift, he told me, from his daughter Brynn, back when she was speaking to him.

There was nothing here of value.

The detectives had left the trash I'd been planning to carry off after my last visit, though they'd clearly opened the bag and searched through it. If there had been anything relevant, they'd have found it, but I still wanted to sift through the mess, perhaps see if Nick had thrown away anything with his wife's address.

What would I tell her that wouldn't get me charged with either stalking or harassment?

I believed Nick was innocent, but I couldn't really *know*, could I? Why would he admit his guilt if doing so might make me stop bringing him food?

The trash bag mostly contained empty boxes of cookies and crackers, some dirty paper plates and paper towels. A couple of unremarkable pieces of mail.

Addressed to Nick Degraff at a P.O. Box in Skyway.

I hadn't seen any rental payments for the box in Nick's account history, but then I'd only looked back three months. He could have paid for six months or even a year in advance.

Stalder and Klimczyk had probably taken another piece of mail with the address and already checked out anything that was waiting for him there. Though it seemed unlikely the murderer would have mailed anything incriminating, expecting it to arrive *after* he committed the murder.

Still, it was the only thing even remotely resembling a clue I'd found. Tomorrow was my day off, and there was no reason not to head to the post office. A new sheet of dinosaur stamps should be on sale. I liked using festive stamps on holiday cards.

Checking the P.O. Box wouldn't be a waste of time in any event because it would show the universe someone still cared about Nick. The universe needed to know it.

"Calling Occupants of Interplanetary Degrees of Glory," I sang softly to myself. It didn't have much of a ring.

I stepped out of the camper and carefully closed the door behind me. There was no way to mask the broken tape.

Oh, well.

"I wondered if you were in there."

Elijah. He knew what I'd been up to. I sighed. Another oh, well. "I was hoping to find a signed confession from the murderer," I quipped a bit listlessly.

"How'd that work out for you?"

"Not too well."

Elijah paused a moment. "Nick told me…" He tapped his foot nervously on a mossy section of sidewalk.

"Yes?"

"He told me about the little…extra favors you did for him."

"Uh huh."

"It's, um, been a pretty stressful day," Elijah went on, "worrying if the killer was still around." He was shirtless despite the rapidly falling temperature now that it was almost dark. His skin was a lovely mocha, with a tattoo of a crab over his left breast. Probably born in July.

He picked casually at his stained, blue sweats.

During his brief, wild period shortly after his mission, Nick had gotten tattoos of the temple markings, a reverse L over his right breast, a V over his left, a flat line over the navel, and another flat line over the knee.

"Every knee shall bow to the Lord."

I nodded. Elijah was unmasked, but there were just some risks you had to take. I walked over and followed him into his camper.

Chapter Seven: Man in the Tattered, Gray Underwear

"You've done this before," Elijah said as he pulled out of my mouth.

"I thought we'd established that before we started."

"You should give lessons." He frowned. "To straight women, I mean."

Like the former head of the KKK who'd written a book under a female pen name, giving advice to women on how to treat their men as they deserved.

"A skill is more valuable when it's rare," I pointed out.

"You gave me all this food, and you made me feel good, so maybe I can give you something." Elijah pulled his sweatpants back up and began rummaging in a frayed cardboard box.

I wasn't sure there was anything in there I'd need. And I definitely didn't want the experience to feel transactional. During all my time escorting, I'd never contracted a single STI. Even with all my casual hook ups, I'd only been diagnosed with a non-specific urethritis once. Crabs, of course, I'd caught many a time.

I looked up at Elijah's tattoo and instinctively touched my beard.

I'd seen an article the other day about a new drug-resistant strain of gonorrhea going around, but I still had no intention of sucking a guy off while he wore a condom.

Elijah held out a white business card. I took it and read "Steven J. Akerstrom, Esq." along with some contact info. Yikes. Had the police told Elijah they suspected me?

"Nick gave me the card. Some pro bono guy from his church. Was supposed to help him with whatever he got up to at work. Nick was never very clear about what he'd done."

"Why did he give this to you?"

Elijah chuckled. "I've got up to some things, too."

I nodded. "Did you show this to the detectives?"

Elijah laughed again. "I don't talk to the police."

***

The post office in Skyway opened at 9:00 a.m., so I was at the bus stop at 8:50. I should have walked to the building instead. The post office was only thirty minutes away and I needed to rev up my metabolism as early in the day as possible. But there was a two-block stretch just before Grocery Outlet without a sidewalk, and with so many drivers looking at their phones, I was afraid of being run over.

Only one problematic passenger on the short ride, an elderly Asian man with his mask down below his chin. He raised his mask only to wipe his nose with it and then pulled the soiled thing back below his chin again.

China was still imposing strict lockdowns and citizens were protesting more and more vehemently. The global population was about to reach eight billion any day now. We almost *needed* a new variant to wipe out two or three billion people. I wasn't sure I minded being part of that group. I simply didn't want to be one of a mere million, a drop of water in a parched California forest.

We could have stopped global warming in time if we'd taken it seriously decades ago. Now the situation was so dire the only option left was a gastric bypass for the climate. Even radical measures might no longer help.

I *wanted* to go on the Arctic Circle expedition, no matter the waste of resources.

I looked longingly at the Grocery Outlet as we passed.

Wouldn't it be nice to have jam and bread again?

I'd written to Maria von Trapp while in college after reading her story. The movie only covered the first couple of chapters. She'd graciously written back, but a few years later, a vengeful ex had gone through my things before moving out and torn it up.

Soon I was at the lower end of Skyway and deboarded. Three police cars were in the parking lot of the convenience store. A black man in tattered gray underwear lay face down on the concrete, a white towel under his head, apparently to make him more comfortable while his hands were cuffed behind his back. He had no other clothing and so couldn't possibly be armed.

We weren't going to have another George Floyd, were we? Another Elijah McClain? Another Eric Garner?

The towel was a hopeful sign, though the murderers from *In Cold Blood* had put pillows under the heads of all four family members before shooting them.

The police cars had their lights flashing, but the officers themselves were standing around calmly, the man on the ground awake but calm as well. The only other thing amiss that I could see was a garbage can that had been turned over in front of the store.

Was this a homelessness issue? A mental health issue? Both?

When Tony and I first started dating, he'd play Matchbox Twenty's "Unwell," saying it reminded him of me. I'd sing him Captain and Tenille.

"Love will keep us together!"

I skirted the parking lot and passed by the bank which had been closed since the beginning of the pandemic. The walk-up ATM had been removed and boarded up two years ago, but the drive-thru ATM had been left intact. Today, though, I noticed warning signs everywhere forbidding anyone from using that ATM as a walk-up location. It was to be removed altogether in the coming days.

Skyway was one of the poorest neighborhoods in Seattle. And now the closest ATM was at least a twenty-minute bus ride away, a branch of this particular bank even farther.

I opened the door to the post office and stood in line. Even this early, there were already six people ahead of me, only one postal employee at the counter, an African immigrant who'd worked here for years.

"Can I help you?"

I held up a piece of Nick's mail. "Mr. Degraff asked me to pick up his mail for him."

"You don't have his key?"

"He's in the hospital." Not technically a lie, since the morgue was probably in the basement.

"He give you his ID? Your name listed on his account?"

"I'm afraid not."

"I can't help you." He looked behind me. "Next!"

"Look," I said, "Nick lives in a camper. Someone broke in and attacked him. I'm just trying to—"

The man shook his head. I nodded back and moved away from the counter. The postal clerk was perfectly right to say no, of course, and there was no point being an ass about it. I already knew the chances of finding anything useful here were slim, even if I did get into his box.

I'd send a notice to the postal service later commending the man for doing his job.

Back outside, I realized I couldn't go to the nearest bus stop, the one in front of the convenience store. An additional police car had arrived, its lights flashing, too, and a paramedic vehicle that said "AID" on the back. The man in gray underwear still lay on the pavement with his head on a towel.

Rosa Wilder often failed in her first attempts to find useful clues, but she generally felt frustrated by those failures. I simply felt like an idiot.

I walked down a block and a half to the next bus stop. It was hot today, unusual for this time of year, though not the 108° we'd had last year, the day a nearby town had burned to the ground. The man in the gray underwear was probably sunburned already. As I waited for the bus, I couldn't take advantage of the bus shelter because of the curve in the road. The driver wouldn't be able to see me in time to stop. Fortunately, there was a community bulletin board that offered partial shade if I crouched down a little. Most of the posters and notices on the board had been ripped off and tossed on the sidewalk.

No ads for hired assassins as far as I could tell.

There were ways, of course, to solicit for illegal activities using euphemisms. Back when I'd been escorting to pay my way through school, I'd advertised as an unlicensed masseur. I hadn't felt delinquent. I'd performed more genuine service then than I ever had as a missionary.

I couldn't stay in touch with my relatives after I left the church because I didn't want to give them ammunition against LGBTQ folks.

Even a lot of gay guys thought I gave gays a bad name.

I had always paid my taxes on the escort income, though, listing it as "Consulting."

Nothing on the bulletin board advertising "discount prescription refills." You couldn't just walk up to someone who "looked" like a druggie and ask, could you?

Over a hundred and fifty homeless people had died in Seattle last year of fentanyl overdoses. Eighty or so more from other kinds of overdoses. Another ten had frozen to death. Seven had committed suicide.

Opioid addiction was a Rorschach test. Some people saw a bunch of bums. Others saw a drug epidemic driven by for-profit pharmaceutical companies.

I still had one more psych appointment to schedule right before the bypass. I wouldn't, of course, be mentioning any of this.

Hard to believe I'd applied to be a store Santa the Christmas before the pandemic for some extra cash.

Not so hard to believe the hiring manager told me I wasn't jolly enough.

"Bah, humbug!" I'd said as I walked out of the interview.

Always a riot.

Another police car headed past toward the convenience store, its lights flashing but its siren silent.

Behind me, a black evangelical church operated out of what looked like a warehouse. Other than the new public library, everything else along this stretch was falling into disrepair. A daycare in a squat, cinder block building housed children playing behind a chain link fence. Across the street was a smoke and beer store, a massage parlor, and an attorney's office specializing in work injuries.

A Spanish language religious bookstore had recently unboarded its windows, though, a hopeful sign, if religious influence could be considered hopeful.

Behind the buildings were majestic firs, spruces, and cedars, hills and mountains in the distance, even snow-covered Mount Rainier, natural sights which should have been breathtaking but which were almost unnoticeable because of all the misery in front of them.

A young Mormon man had killed five people at a gay club in Colorado the other day. His father had been relieved to learn his son wasn't gay, that "all" he'd done was kill people.

Fifteen minutes later, the bus pulled up. I'd been gone almost an hour for an errand I didn't even get to complete. In some ways, this was an everyday event. Trivial. Not worth mentioning. In other ways, it felt almost traumatizing to witness so much misery on this many levels, amplified precisely because the misery was so easily ignored by anyone who wasn't experiencing it.

But how could anyone be traumatized by a normal day?

Nick mattered, I told myself, my jaw clenching. I wasn't going home. I was heading straight for light rail. It was time to talk to Nick's boss.

Chapter Eight: A Cackle of Karens

Light rail was usually nicer than the bus but not today. Several tourists were headed downtown with their suitcases, taking up twice as much space as they needed. Tourists sometimes defiantly claimed their space, daring anyone to claim an empty seat. These particular folks simply looked oblivious to the needs of others, chattering away happily, probably in town for a game.

One of the men wore a T-shirt with an image of a rifle and the words "Come and get it!" while his friend wore one with an image of a rainbow flag surrounded by a red circle with a slash through it. Their wives wore T-shirts equally as dangerous. One shirt read "It's not a crime to be better than others" and the other read "We know who you are and we know where you live."

It was impossible to distinguish parody from reality anymore, with one prominent right-wing politician calling for a ban on blasphemy, another accusing Deep State Commies of using secret technology to send hurricanes to red states.

One of the tourists coughed. None of the group was masked.

The Asian, Latin, and Middle Eastern passengers on board pretended not to notice them. So did the other white passengers.

Though I could ignore an elephant in the living room with the best of them, I'd grown tired of doing so. Tony hated when I went to white supremacist rallies as a counterprotester. "You'll get shot," he said, "and then where will I be? I'll have to pay the mortgage by myself!"

But was there anything to do about these jerks on the train? What could I say?

I was weighing my options when the light rail stopped at Columbia City and a very drunk white man in his early twenties boarded, wearing filthy jeans that hung so low I could see he was going commando. His treasure trail was annoyingly tempting despite the grime. He grabbed onto a bar as we took off, trying to focus long enough to find a place to sit. When he saw the tourists glaring at him, he smiled, waved, and then hit himself in the stomach.

I watched as he spewed all over both men and one of the women. The other woman managed to escape. But they all shouted.

I couldn't help but laugh. And then I clapped, not caring in the least if I was being a jerk. Which probably meant I was. Most of the other riders still pretended they hadn't noticed anyone else on board, but two others clapped as well, a young black woman and an Indian man in his thirties.

"You people are sick!" the soiled woman shouted. "We're never coming back to Seattle again!"

"Promise?" a white passenger asked calmly.

The vomiter knew when to make his exit, though, jogging down to the end of the attached car and deboarding at the next stop.

***

In a better mood now, I climbed the steps from the Pioneer Station platform up to 3rd Avenue. A City employee had been hit in the head with a hammer here a couple of weeks earlier while trying to reach street level. The elevators never worked. I climbed up the steep hill to 4th, urging my metabolism to gear up. Then I passed a Starbucks where workers were striking in protest of union busting and made my way north a couple more blocks.

One sign read, "If the only way you can stay in business is to pay starvation wages, you're admitting up front that capitalism doesn't work."

The front of another sign read, "Do you know what would happen if the richest people in the world were forced to pay taxes?" The back of the sign read, "They'd still be the richest people in the world."

Most people didn't know the labor history of Seattle, going back more than a hundred years. Schools certainly didn't teach it.

Deception was the name of the game, though, and I wasn't bad at it myself.

As a missionary in Rome, I'd been taught all kinds of subterfuge. We'd ring at the citofono outside the main door of a palazzo, button after button, until someone let us inside. Then we'd knock on every door in the building. We'd memorize a name from the list out front so that if there was a portiere monitoring the place, we could say something like, "Oh, Signor Malatesta asked us to come talk to him."

If a woman said no at her door, we'd use her name at the next. "Signora Cozzolino said you might be interested."

We called it "lying for the Lord." It wasn't an original invention. Many right-wing politicians across the U.S. and elsewhere practiced the same philosophy.

So when I reached the fourth floor of the building that I hoped housed Nick's former employer, I walked up to the receptionist confidently.

"Hi! Can I help you?" she asked. The nameplate on her desk read "Elodie Bliquez."

The young woman was in her mid-twenties, white, with jet black hair cut in a bob. Not a tattoo anywhere to be seen, her attire crisp and professional.

"I need to speak to HR about Nick Degraff."

It would have helped if I'd worn a suit rather than come directly from the post office, but the truth was it had been three or four years since I last fit into my suit. I could hardly afford to purchase one just for my "investigation." Thank goodness my jeans weren't faded and my polo shirt wasn't frayed.

"Oh!" the young woman said, blinking. "I—I—"

At least she seemed to recognize the name. I'd guessed right when looking up possible names for the company as Valentina had suggested.

Miss Bliquez looked off down the hall behind her and then back at me. "I'm afraid our HR manager isn't in today."

"I see." Her nervous blinking made me doubt the claim. "Can I make an appointment?" I could tell Joshua I had a dental appointment if I needed to come back on a day I was scheduled to work.

Miss Bliquez started to speak, stopped, and then took a breath. "I'm afraid all of that is being handled by our legal team."

"Can I speak to someone on the legal team?"

"I'm afraid not." The young woman had completely regained her composure. There was no longer any hesitation in her replies. The visit was over.

"Well, thank you for your time, miss," I said, nodding my head in parting. That was that. God only knows what I would have asked anyway, or what good it would have done. If the receptionist could stonewall at this level, the HR manager or legal team surely could, too.

As I started to turn away, though, the receptionist revealed she was in fact still uncomfortable when she nervously brushed her hair behind her ear. My eyes widened involuntarily.

"What?" she said, almost defensively.

"Those dragonfly earrings are *spectacular*." I nodded again and then continued on my way. At least I hadn't said "fabulous." I wasn't *that* gay.

I had just pulled the door open to the hallway when I heard, "Wait a sec." A moment later, I was following Elodie toward the HR manager's office.

The floor layout suggested this wasn't the most pleasant company to work for. Offices for important employees lined the outer walls so that only they had access to windows or views. Everyone else sat in cubicles in the middle. That would have been bad enough, but the cubicle employees weren't even granted much in the way of cubicle walls, all of the partitions rising only eighteen inches above their desks. It allowed some minor bulletin board functionality but never allowed anyone to so much as pick their nose without being seen by everyone else.

As missionaries, we'd been ordered to stay with our companions twenty-four hours a day. We ate together, shopped together, worked together, spent our one day off together. If we were lucky, we got to shower or shit in peace. But with six elders to an apartment, even that wasn't a given.

Despite the lack of visual obstructions in the office, as we passed one pathway between cubicles, an employee rushed out without looking, almost running into the receptionist. She stopped just in time, I almost ran into her, and the man instead bumped into a custodian, who dropped a trash can he was emptying. Some of its contents spilled onto the floor.

The man from the cubicles didn't apologize but went on about his business. Elodie turned to me and waved me to continue following.

My mother had told me when I was a teen to watch the way people treated those they considered beneath them because one day they'd treat me the same way.

I bent down for just a moment to help the custodian gather the trash back into the can and then joined Elodie again.

I truly understood when people didn't have the strength or commitment to do difficult things. But easy ones? I could be the patron saint of Piddly Efforts.

I remembered the tight jeans on the man in the "King of Wishful Thinking" video.

Nick's former company had control of the entire floor, and Human Resources occupied one of the back corners. Before she knocked on the door, Elodie turned back to me once more. "Erik can be a bit...intense," she whispered, "but he's a good man."

Reassuring.

Elodie rapped on the door, and when someone inside shouted, "Come in!" she pushed it open.

"Erik," she began.

"Mr. Marklund," he corrected.

"Excuse me, Mr. Marklund, this gentleman would like to speak to you about Mr. Degraff."

Erik—Mr. Marklund—looked at us both with what could only be described as "a stony expression." Hard, cold, impassive. The only other time I'd seen such a look was on the face of one of my zone leaders in Naples when I talked back to him in district meeting in front of the other missionaries.

Though I supposed I'd worn a similar expression myself the day I almost pushed Elder Higgins off our fifth-floor balcony after he forced me to spend three hours struggling to recite the H discussion before I was ready and then still refused to pass me.

"I'm working with Nick's attorney," I said, "Mr. Akerstrom." I nodded officiously. "We'd like to see Mr.

Degraff's personnel file. Read the complaints and the various actions taken. The sequence of events." A real request would have come in the form of an official letter, maybe even delivered by courier.

Mr. Marklund stood up slowly and walked toward us. Elodie took a tiny step back. "Why did you bring him here?" he demanded.

Elodie took a quick breath and regained her footing. "Well, he asked to see you," she said, "and it's your job to—"

"I know how to do my job," he said coolly. "Why don't you do yours?"

This was not going at all as I had planned. Perhaps—

"Why don't you ever notice my earrings?" the receptionist asked.

Mr. Marklund's eyes moved from Elodie's face to mine without ever diverting to her ears. "Because I'm not a fucking faggot!" he spat.

"To be fair," I interrupted, "I don't get the opportunity to fuck nearly as often as I'd like these days."

Elodie took two larger steps back now. I could barely see her in my peripheral vision. But what did I care what the head of HR thought? What was he going to do? Report me to Nick's attorney?

It was easy to be brave when you had nothing at stake.

Though I realized I was doing the same thing I'd done with the detectives. And antagonizing this man wouldn't get me the answers I wanted.

"Get lost, you fat mutherfucker."

"I've actually always preferred daddy types," I said. "And you're far too femme to have any cause to worry."

Mr. Marklund took another step in my direction, and I heard Elodie gasp somewhere behind me. How did these things escalate so quickly? I was lucky not to be a black man being questioned during a routine traffic stop.

Marklund lowered his face into mine. "Drop dead."

I waited as he waited for me to retreat. "You must have been valedictorian at your charm school." I continued looking into his face without lowering my eyes.

I wondered if the man was truly homophobic or if he was simply using my orientation as justification for denying my request to see the records. Though I supposed the options weren't mutually exclusive.

Mr. Marklund put his hand on my chest, pushed me out of his office, and slammed the door. I could hear the lock click. I turned toward the receptionist.

"I am so sorry!" she said. "My boyfriend—I mean, Mr. Marklund—can get a little…"

"Don't apologize," I told her. "I put you in an awkward position." I took a breath. "I'm the one who needs to apologize." While I might not have had anything to lose, she did, and I shouldn't be realizing that only now.

Why couldn't I do the easy things?

I followed Elodie back to her desk. She sat down, moved a few papers nervously, and fluffed her hair.

"I'm sorry," I said, realizing I hadn't actually apologized yet.

"It's not your fault."

"I've seen healthier work cultures," I admitted. And I understood a little better why cops felt tempted to use their power to force answers from folks who refused to cooperate.

Absolute power corrupted absolutely. Maybe that was why the God so many people followed seemed like an asshole.

Elodie shrugged.

"I hope the rest of your day goes better." I started toward the door. "And Miss Bliquez?"

"Yes?"

"You deserve to be with someone who notices your earrings."

Chapter Nine: A Chaos of Clues

When I arrived back at the Pioneer Square station, a muffled voice from the speaker informed me that an accident somewhere up ahead had delayed the train indefinitely. I climbed back up to the street and walked over to Jackson where I hoped to catch either the 106 or the 7.

The scene on 12th made Skyway look like the suburbs.

This had always been a rough area, but it had deteriorated a great deal in the past few years. Half the stores were closed and boarded up, graffiti covering the walls of both the closed and operating businesses. Parking lots were fenced off, some with both barbed wire and razor wire on top. There was trash everywhere, pigeon droppings covering the sidewalk every inch or two, competing with dried—and sometimes wet—vomit for prominence.

Dirty, haggard men wearing ill-fitting clothes walked past carrying stolen goods in new boxes right from the store, items they clearly were not in a position to buy, televisions, mostly, and other electronics. Some of the porters argued and cursed each other. Some approached folks waiting for the bus. One middle-aged Asian woman clutched her purse tightly and kept running away but then returned to wait for the bus again, then ran away once more when someone else approached her.

A white woman around forty was hunched over, her legs bent, her head down, as if trying hard to stay awake but only seconds away from collapsing. She kept shrinking closer and closer to the ground, teetering and tottering. She was surely going to smash her face into a fresh patch of vomit, but she refused to sit, jerking back awake and straightening up again for only a few seconds before starting slowly to shrink down once more, over and over the entire fifteen minutes I waited. A heavyset black man in a filthy car pulled over and called out to her to get in. He called and called, louder and louder, but she was oblivious and he finally drove on.

I finally decided to head to the International District station, grateful to see a train departing as I reached the platform. At least they were running again.

Light rail wasn't overly crowded as I headed back south. A lone, dirty shoe rested on one seat, while nearby seats showcased a nearly empty tub of macaroni and an empty carton of ice cream. I hardly paid attention as a white man with a beard—and no mask—walked past me down the aisle and sat somewhere behind me. He wore black jeans and a T-shirt that read "Antisocial Social Club."

Okay, so I noticed. He had a big box.

I was a detective, after all. I noticed things.

When I'd read *The Wizard of Oz* as a teen, I'd been surprised to see how different it was from the 1939 movie. The Emerald City wasn't even green. Everyone was simply required by law to wear green glasses, so they *thought* the city was green.

What was the color, I wondered, of unhappiness? Maybe folks with synesthesia saw a variety of colors. A spectrum.

Like transition lenses that darkened when exposed to bright sunlight, my exposure to increasing unhappiness kept changing the way I perceived the world. I couldn't even tell if I was projecting or not. Perhaps everyone else wasn't nearly as miserable as I thought they were. A recent article claimed that Seattle was ranked fifteenth in happiest American cities.

I heard a loud puff and then felt as well as saw clouds of smoke passing along both sides of my face. The guy behind me was smoking.

I turned around. "Aren't *you* impressive?" I asked.

The man jumped to his feet and glared down at me. "I'm gonna fuck you up!" he shouted. "Who the fuck do you think you are, talking to me like that!"

"I'm an antisocial butterfly," I explained.

The man slapped the top of the seat next to me. The fact that I wasn't afraid probably spoke more to my growing depression than my bravery.

"I take it back," I said. "You're not impressive. You're boring." Then I turned back around.

The man continued shouting and cursing and slapping the seat. I looked forward, tilting my head slightly as if dozing in an attempt to illustrate my lack of concern. If he hadn't hit me yet, though, he wasn't likely to.

Had Nick's attacker struck out for something just as random and pointless?

Whenever people read of someone's death, that of a celebrity or relative or coworker, our first question was always, "What did they die of?" We wanted to know. But did it make any difference?

"Oh, she died of lung cancer. And she didn't even smoke. How sad." As if dying of lung cancer because you did smoke was somehow okay, when tobacco companies who knew of the dangers deliberately made cigarettes more addictive.

What would change really if I found out who killed Nick?

The train pulled into the next station, and the antisocial social club member stormed off.

It mattered, I thought, because even if it was random, the murderer could kill again.

***

I couldn't face walking all the way uphill and so waited sixteen minutes for the 106 on Henderson, but I did manage to deboard two stops early, hoping to burn a handful of extra calories. I remembered my stake president telling my father after I received my mission call to Italy, "Morgan's going to be one of those young men who comes back from his mission fat." He clearly didn't know much about the Italy Rome Mission. Our mission president forbid us from eating pasta more than twice a week, and we either rode the bus or walked everywhere we went. I returned to America two years later in the best shape of my life.

18% body fat.

My stake president had been called as a General Authority while I was away.

I had 39% body fat now.

The bus stop along this stretch of Renton was barely visible from the street, squeezed in between two campers, but the drivers knew where it was. I paused by Elijah's door briefly. I didn't want the man to think I was after sex. I hadn't brought any food or other supplies, and I'd just seen the guy yesterday, but I hadn't had much opportunity to talk to him about Nick.

In TV shows, detectives often learned something new when interviewing suspects or witnesses a second or third time. Imma Tataranni, for instance, was usually preoccupied with her feelings for her much younger coworker or worrying about her husband having an affair and so didn't always focus as she should.

I knocked on Elijah's door, and he opened it a moment later. His eyes darted down to my hands and then the sidewalk, searching for food.

"I'm sorry," I said. "I'm just coming back from downtown and thought I'd give you an update. I went to Nick's workplace to try to find out a little more, but no one wanted to talk."

"Did you try blowing them?"

"The opportunity didn't present itself."

"Sometimes, you have to make your own opportunities."

It was sage advice but I felt awkward hearing it from a homeless man. It reminded me of the video clip I'd seen of the new Prime Minister in the UK "volunteering" at a homeless shelter as a PR stunt. A man had come up for a plate of food, and the Prime Minister tried to sound folksy and start up a conversation. "So...do you have a business in the area?"

"Uh, no," the man had replied. "I'm homeless."

"If you want to suck my dick again," Elijah said, "I won't say no."

It was going to be difficult to get much additional questioning in. As I knelt beside the frayed box from the day before, I watched Elijah pull down his sweats and noticed something I'd missed during our last encounter. He was wearing Nick's CTR ring on his index finger.

The T in the middle was the largest letter, rising above and dropping below the letters on either side, so it was difficult to know if the T was the first letter, middle, or last letter of the three.

"Choose the Right" was one of several Mormon mottos, and I'd never seen Nick without that ring on his hand. If he'd been wearing it when he was murdered, the police would have it, or it would at least be in some drawer or bag at the coroner's office.

Elijah paused, and when I looked up at him, I could see he realized I'd recognized the ring. "Nick gave it to me the day before he was killed," he said. "Said I should have a ring to remind me about Critical Race Theory." He chuckled. "I don't need a white man to talk to me about race, but I like the ring."

I could think of half a dozen reasons Elijah might have that ring, some good, some bad, some damning. And it was only one single "clue." I was ignorant of probably three dozen others Stalder and Klimczyk had gathered. How anyone made sense of the whole mess was beyond me.

There was a reason detectives went through professional training.

I needed to stick to what I knew.

I pulled down Elijah's sweats and got to work. He grabbed the back of my head and pulled my face forcefully into his crotch, pumping away like his life depended on it.

A lesser man might have choked. Or at least gagged. But I was, after all, a pro.

***

This last part of the hill was the steepest, so I walked slowly. There was a beautiful spruce across Renton at the next stop, a spectacular redwood two houses down on a side street.

A dead raccoon lay in the bicycle lane. Two crows on a telephone wire above seemed to be discussing its death rather heatedly.

Last week—was it only a week ago?—Nick had told me about a homeless man near his workplace who sat on the same corner every day. Sometimes, the man held out a sign asking for food. Other times, he dozed while people walked past. One morning, noticing a worse than usual odor, one of Nick's coworkers had paused just long enough to realize the guy was dead.

Nick said the coroner determined he'd been dead at least five days.

I wondered if Elodie had been the one who finally stopped to check.

When I got home, I looked up Steven J. Akerstrom's office and sent an email. I simply wasn't up to talking to anyone else today about the case. I almost hoped no one would respond. This would be the end of my amateurish investigation, and I could finally move on.

But to what?

When I was younger, I accepted problems and obstacles. They were part of paying my dues. They'd be inspiring details in my success story. Suffering was bearable if it ultimately led to something good.

That was Mormon theology. It was the American Dream. Toxic positivity.

My attitude changed, though, when I realized the problems and obstacles weren't part of the journey. They were the destination.

Things were never going to get better.

Doomscrolling didn't help, but it was my one vice. I looked at headlines on Yahoo twice a day, watched short news clips on YouTube. It was important to be informed, to be aware of the rest of the planet.

But that meant watching a report on the Nord Stream pipeline being sabotaged in the Baltic Sea, Putin threatening nuclear war again, Trump defending the discovery of top secret documents in his Florida home by declaring he could declassify them with his mind.

It meant watching conservatives ask insurance companies to stop covering PreP.

After I was excommunicated, I'd volunteered at Harborview, back in the days when men were going blind and developing dementia at twenty-five.

Right-wing politicians might not round us up into camps when they gained total control of the government, but they could still make sure we suffered or died, the way both parties already did for millions of black people. The U.S. already housed two million prisoners. Why not a million more?

Private prisons helped the economy.

I clicked on a video showing a right-wing news host claiming that the left wanted everyone to mate with dwarfs to combat climate change. And I kept watching videos the rest of the afternoon.

I heard the front door open and went to greet Tony with a kiss. "How was work?" I asked.

"Don't ask."

I nodded and headed to the kitchen to whip up a batch of chaffles for us both.

"Jesus Christ, Morgan!" I heard from the bedroom. "You had the whole day off and couldn't be bothered to do laundry?"

I left the bowl of egg and cheese on the counter and met Tony in the living room. "Well?" he demanded.

"I guess you'll have to stay home from work tomorrow." I shrugged. "You do get eight hours of emergency leave, don't you?"

Tony left for dinner and a sleepover with a friend. I cooked up three chaffles and then sat down for another episode of *The Bastards of Pizzofalcone*.

God, it was annoying when the detectives took a phone call in the middle of an important conversation and ran off to save the day. Sometimes, I just wanted to reach into the television and smack someone upside the head.

Chapter Ten: A Cacophony of Creeps

This morning's doomscrolling revealed that a former National Security Adviser claimed that "Israelis" were trying to inject robots into Americans though vaccines to turn us all into cyborgs. Several right-wing politicians were calling for Christian nationalism. Iran was threatening to execute thousands of people who protested the Morality Police killing of a young woman for not covering her head properly.

A man three blocks from my house in Rainier Beach had been shot in the neck at 10:00 last night, the perpetrator shooting from outside and through the man's window.

I drank a cup of protein shake from my shaker bottle and headed to work.

The 106 wasn't overly crowded this morning, but there were still few places to sit. Most of the empty seats had trash littered across them. Other seats were wet, though it wasn't raining. No one wanted to take a chance on finding out what kind of liquid had soiled the seats.

A homeless woman lay across the seats along the back row, eating cheese crisps.

Impoverished people marked their territory as they could, like cats, like dogs, like wolves. "I was here!"

"I *am* here!"

Understanding why someone did something annoying, unfortunately, did little to decrease the annoyance. If it did, I wouldn't be so annoyed with myself all the time.

Why hadn't I planned my trip to Nick's workplace better? Why hadn't I asked Elijah better questions?

Why hadn't I been able to win Nick's trust so he could tell me what had happened at work? Find a way to help him clear his name?

I'd bought him a goddamn box of raisin crème pies.

Like sex, providing food was more service than I'd given as a missionary. But the man needed something even more fundamental. And I'd failed him.

A cousin I followed minimally on social media routinely posted that empathy was overrated, that it made people weak. He was still an active Mormon. But anti-empathy attitudes seemed to be the prevailing philosophy of many folks these days.

The next time someone used "antifa" as a slur, I'd label the accusers "anti-em" instead.

But maybe they had a point. If I focused on the cruelties inflicted on Judy Garland—or even Margaret Hamilton—during the filming of *The Wizard of Oz*, I'd never enjoy watching the movie again. And I wanted to enjoy it.

I looked out the window as the bus drove along MLK. The firs and spruces and redwoods never failed to astonish me, so beautiful. And there were other signs of beauty, too, restaurants and bookstores and life all around. Even if large parts of the city were filled with poor and homeless folks, Seattle could still be a great place to live.

Except that as a diabetic, I couldn't eat at any of those restaurants, even if I had money. And as a poor person, I still couldn't eat at any of those restaurants, even if I wasn't diabetic. I was an outsider, a prisoner walking among the free.

Mannaggia.

A drama queen, I supposed, without any crown jewels.

I needed to make an appointment as soon as my surgery was completed and get in at least three therapy sessions while I could.

Mirelle greeted me with a smile when I arrived at the bank, pulling her hair back to reveal a new pair of earrings.

"Are those pangolins?" I asked.

"Yes!" She laughed. "I knew you'd know!"

"They're absolutely lovely."

"Thank you."

Jevin told me he was doing well in his Fantasy Football League, and I quipped that I'd made it to the finals in my Fantasy Karaoke League. Joshua reminded me I wasn't being paid to practice my stand-up routine.

A shame, because mine sure needed practice.

The rest of the morning went reasonably well. One woman deposited lots of fives, tens, and twenties totaling $635. We'd been told to fill out a Suspicious Activity Report for such transactions, but the transaction only struck me as suspicious from the perspective of someone with financially stable family and friends.

The small bills could have been drug money, of course, or the woman might have earned them the way I had back in the day. But she could also have earned the money dancing. Or playing her guitar at Westlake. The woman was entitled to some privacy.

I remembered a news report about the Attorney General in Texas trying to get a law passed allowing him to extradite parents of trans kids who'd escaped the state so he could prosecute them even after they'd moved to a state that didn't criminalize transition therapy.

Cutting off two-thirds of my stomach wasn't going to be enough. I needed to remove two-thirds of my thoughts as well.

Hopefully, without a lobotomy.

Another young woman gifted me some homemade cookies while I completed her transaction. It felt odd to be a grandfather figure. In my head, I was still thirty-five. And simultaneously sixty-one. And ninety-three. I handed the plate of cookies to Mirelle when she went on her lunch.

I supposed I should have brought them home to Tony. I needed to do more to repair our relationship, focus on things I actually had some power over. And there were so many other ways I fell short. Even my attempts at self-education turned into doomscrolling.

A disturbing video I'd watched last night explained that our brains reset when we gained weight so that we kept the same number of fat cells. I already knew that we never lost those cells, that they simply got smaller as we dropped pounds, but I hadn't realized that once fat cells eventually died after nine or ten years, our brains insisted on replacing them, even if we were eating moderately. Far more shocking was the revelation that even if we were able to afford liposuction and physically remove 60% of the offending cells, our brain *still* forced our bodies to replace them. That higher number of fat cells was a constant, only changing if we gained more weight and that steady number rose.

The change only went in one direction.

Kind of like politics, with the right moving farther right, the left moving toward the center, and the center moving toward the right.

Every day, I felt like Ulysses on a death-defying adventure. But I was merely Sisyphus trying to toss a half pound stone.

"I can help you over here," I called out to the man at the front of the line.

A gentleman around forty walked up and frowned. I got a lot of frowns, though. The guy was probably an anti-masker. He handed me a check and his ID, and I pulled up his account. Harold Gustafson.

"Could you deposit that in my checking?" he asked.

"Sure thing."

As I typed some information into the computer, my eyes finally focused on the maker. The check had been issued by the company Nick worked for. I looked back up at the customer. It was the custodian.

"So you don't really work for Mr. Degraff's attorney, do you?" Mr. Gustafson asked.

Yikes. "I was a friend of Nick's," I said. "I met him after he became homeless."

Mr. Gustafson shook his head. "Mr. Degraff wasn't perfect. He could be snippy at times." He looked to his left and right to make sure no one could hear him. "But he didn't sign that contract that lost the company all that money."

"Excuse me?"

"I know his handwriting. And someone threw away several sheets of paper with his signature."

"I don't—"

"Someone was practicing."

I nodded, my heart racing so much I wasn't sure I could ask anything useful. "Did...did you save any of the papers?"

Mr. Gustafson shook his head.

"Whose trashcan—?" I stopped myself. Why wouldn't those sheets have been shredded instead of thrown away? Criminals weren't that stupid.

The custodian shook his head again. Did he not know the answer, I wondered? Or...?

I immediately thought about the nasty Mr. Marklund. *He* might have been too hot-headed to think clearly enough to use a shredder, but he was in HR. Whoever signed the contract would need to be another employee on Nick's level. In the same position. Perhaps I could look up a list of employees online.

At the very least, I had something to pass on to Stalder and Klimczyk.

Only they'd want proof, and there was none. And if they went down to the worksite to talk to Mr. Gustafson, their visit could jeopardize his safety.

What would Annika Bengtzon do?

I handed Mr. Gustafson his receipt. And then jotted down my name and number on a slip of scrap paper. He nervously shoved it into his pocket and walked away.

"Are you trying to pick up guys at work?" Joshua demanded. He'd apparently been watching the last part of the transaction.

"We're both friends of the man who was murdered in my neighborhood the other day."

"Morgan, you need to keep your personal and professional life separate."

"Sure thing." I waved the next customer over to my window.

He was a former client who didn't even recognize me because I'd gained so much weight.

Chapter Eleven: A Conundrum of Concerns

During lunch, I managed to tune out Shanifer and Gurkirat successfully. Krichelle texted and asked if I could stop by again.

"You OK?" I texted back.

"Nothing a friendly face and a good game of Scrabble can't fix."

"I'm at lunch if you need to talk."

The phone rang three seconds later.

"Morgan," Krichelle said, "you have time to listen to me kvetch for a while?"

"Is Roger still upset about you writing 'mildewy' on a triple word score the other day?"

"It's about work." I could hear her sigh, even though she pulled the phone away first.

"What's up?"

"My principal demanded we take down a quote we had posted in the library."

Not here in Seattle, too, I thought, pulling my own phone away before I groaned too loudly. "Race?" I asked. "Trans?"

Books like *Maus* and *Boy Shattered* were being banned from more and more school libraries across the country. Some right-wing politicians were even calling for an outright ban on public libraries, closing off public access to all books, not just those with sexual or racial content. Schoolteachers not complying could be charged with felonies or threatened with the label of sex offender.

"It was a quote from Elie Wiesel, for God's sake. You know the one. Let me read it. I took a picture before the librarian took it down."

Libraries had virtually become homeless shelters over the past few years. There was nowhere else for folks to come in out of the rain.

I thought about offering to write an op-ed against book banning, but I couldn't really, could I? No one wanted to become another target. Enraged parents were threatening school board members across the country, showing up at the homes of "liberals," leaving death threats on voice mail.

Krichelle took a breath. "'I swore never to be silent whenever and wherever human beings endure suffering and humiliation. We must always take sides. Neutrality helps the oppressor, never the victim. Silence encourages the tormentor, never the tormented.'"

"Yep, I know it." I used to have the words posted over my PC until I replaced them with Toni Morrison.

Tony had a photo of a naked, erect man over his home computer. Perhaps he had the right idea. At the very least, I should put up a picture of a mountain stream, maybe a field of poppies.

"Can you imagine anyone finding that offensive?" Krichelle continued.

My answer was yes once more, but this time I didn't voice it. A few weeks ago, I'd seen on the news that a white City of Seattle employee was suing the City for creating a hostile work environment by assigning every employee training on implicit bias.

It wasn't ignorance and bias itself I found upsetting. Everyone was ignorant and biased about something, usually many somethings. It was the fact that so many people chose to glorify that ignorance and bias.

"The glory of God is intelligence," Mormon scripture proclaimed. BYU's motto was "The world is our campus."

Even Nick considered himself "different" from other homeless folks.

My former missionary colleagues made fun of Greta Thunberg. Several were proud anti-vaxxers. They praised Putin for banning LGBTQ "propaganda."

These things used to irritate me. Now they frightened me.

"Any words of encouragement?" Krichelle asked.

"It wouldn't hurt," I said slowly, "for you and Roger and Valentina to spend some time studying another language."

Krichelle sighed again, this time right into the phone. "We already let Valentina pick," she said. "We'd hoped for Spanish so we'd have more options, but she wanted German, and we couldn't tell her why we were adding this 'family activity,' so German it is."

Were we freaks, I wondered? Or were other families across America feeling the same sense of foreboding?

I was exceptionally skilled at worrying, of course. Years of honing my craft. And somehow, being old changed my perspective. When I was young, I always felt I could overcome whatever I needed to. Now I understood how easy it was to be crushed.

Even those who followed societal norms, like Nick, could lose everything in an instant.

"I'll write you a list of some good shows you can watch together," I said. A couple I followed were too dark, but I thought they might enjoy *The Weissensee Saga* or *Inspector Dupin*. Maybe even *Homicide Unit Istanbul*. The latter two shows weren't set in Germany but were filmed with German-speaking actors.

People talked about being on the right side of history or being in the right political party or belonging to the right religion. But couldn't we at least choose to be on the right side of humanity?

If only I could get a job with RAI as an English subtitle writer.

"Thanks, Morgan," Krichelle said. "Hopefully…"

"Yes," I agreed. "Hopefully."

"Self-test and see you at 7:00?"

"I'll bring some seltzer water."

I still had three and a half hours after lunch to muddle through. My mind continued to race throughout every transaction. I understood why some people couldn't get out of bed. "Be brave," I told myself. "You're likely to make mistakes, but be brave anyway."

Were brave people scared and depressed all the time?

Just after 3:00, Mirelle called a customer to her window but he deferred, sending the woman behind him to her window instead. The man then came over to me when I was free. "Ciao, Morgan!"

It was Filippo. He'd lived in Seattle for over ten years but was originally from Milano. "Come stai?" I asked as he handed me a check for deposit. He was one of two Italian regulars at our branch. Neither one knew the other.

"Insomma." He shrugged. Filippo always spoke slowly, overenunciating, acting like I was a child, but at least he never switched to English in the middle of a conversation.

I nodded. "Cosa pensi di Giorgia Meloni?"

"Non ne sono contento," he said.

I handed him his receipt. "Se i Trumpisti vincono qui," I told him, "io speravo di scappare in Italia. Ma ora non posso."

He didn't laugh. The far right had made huge strides in Sweden, too. And in Hungary and Turkey and Israel and too many other countries.

"Ci vediamo, Morgan." And then he was gone. The man wasn't even gay, and I wanted to leave with him. Talk him into asking a family member in Italy to rent me a room, even with the growing fascism there.

Was it time to learn a third language?

In Napoli, Elder Welty and I had found ourselves teaching a man who told us he was a Communist. At the time, I'd been afraid we might be struck by lightning for not immediately walking out of his apartment. I'd thought

Communists were all on the other side of the Iron Curtain, not realizing that 30% of Italians were registered with the Party. We'd watched a Communist rally marching up Via Roma after church one Sunday.

And there was almost always one sciopero or another. When bus drivers went on strike once in the middle of the day, we had to walk ninety minutes to get back home.

Elder Welty tried to convert Gennaro to capitalism, and it was only then I realized that nothing in the Bible declared capitalism ordained of God. The economic system didn't even exist until hundreds of years later. Nothing in the Book of Mormon proclaimed it "The One True Economic Policy," either.

I'd always just assumed it was in there, the way people assumed Genesis talked about apples.

"Anziano Beylerian," Gennaro asked me on our last visit, "if you stole your neighbor's TV, would that be wrong?"

"Yes."

"Would it be wrong if your neighbor stole *your* TV?"

"Obviously."

"If you took ₺20,000 from the cash register at work, what would happen?" About $20 at the time, back when Italy still used lire.

"I'd get fired."

"Or arrested," Gennaro said. "And you'd go to prison if you embezzled Ł20,000,000, wouldn't you?"

"I'd never do that."

"So why is it okay if your employer steals from you?"

"We're here to teach, not to learn," Elder Welty had said, grabbing my arm and leading me to the door. We were taught to say just that in the Missionary Training Center if we ever found ourselves in difficulty.

But I'd let my companion exit first, giving Gennaro a thankful nod on my way out. Who knew that it would be during the most righteous period of my life when I'd start questioning righteousness?

"I'm not paying you to take language lessons," Joshua said. He peered over the top of the bullet-proof glass.

I stared directly at him so long he turned around and walked off. It was either that or call him a stronzo, and he might have looked the word up.

"Actually," Mirelle said from her station, "that sounds like a good idea."

"We'd be much better at our job," Jevin joined in, "if we spoke Spanish and Tagalog and Russian."

"I'd settle for not hearing Joshua say shitty things in English," I said.

"Oh, don't let it get to you," Mirelle told me. "Ignore him." She giggled. "I'll put 'language lessons' in the Suggestion Box."

I nodded and called over the next customer. I knew my coworker meant well but still found her advice mildly irritating. It was one reason I spoke so little to Tony these days. "Stop being affected by everything" was his go-to counsel. But it was like saying to an abused spouse, "Don't get bruised when he hits you." Abuse was abusive, even if it was "only" verbal or emotional. And it took a real, not imaginary, toll.

We were pretty much all dealing with institutional abuse, from bosses, from corporations, from religious fanatics, and from "liberal" politicians who couldn't even manage to *vote* for expanding the child tax credit, much less pass a bill to make it a reality.

These things weren't merely news stories, they weren't op-ed pieces or talking points. They were our lives.

If I could solve the mystery of how to make the world a better place, I'd really be onto something.

Joshua saw us talking and headed back over. "I'm not paying you to be friends," he said. "Just do your job."

"A parrot could do yours," I replied, "and would cost the bank a lot less."

Okay, so I didn't really say that. I simply *wanted* to. I suppose it was a victory I finally managed to control myself.

Only keeping my mouth shut didn't feel any better than saying something completely reckless.

***

On my way home, I closed my eyes and dozed. At least three people on board the bus were coughing non-stop. My psyche felt like a glass filled with water almost to the brim. It never took more than a few drops to make the glass overflow.

Why did *everything* irritate me?

Suddenly, I heard a sharp crack, followed by two women screaming. I opened my eyes to see a bullet hole in the window beside the seat in front of me. The driver kept driving another two blocks, but fortunately there were no more shots.

No one had been hurt, thank goodness, and after the driver surveyed the damage, she called in a report. We waited to board the next bus and continued our journey home.

Chapter Twelve: Treasures We Throw Away

I deboarded three stops early but was already tired by the time I'd walked just one bus stop up the hill, pausing when I reached the side street leading to Takahashi Gardens. I debated whether or not to detour for a few minutes of contemplation beside the waterfall. The garden entrance was uphill in a different direction, though, meaning I'd have to come back downhill again before heading back uphill to get home.

Just before I could cross the side street and continue on home, a car turned in off Renton, and I caught the driver's eye. It was Tockner, off duty, apparently. The debate was over. I changed direction and walked the rest of the way to the small parking lot in front of the garden. Tockner stood beside his car, waiting. He lived somewhere nearby but would never specify where.

"Long time, no suck," he said.

"We should probably do something about that."

"Any suggestions?"

I shrugged. "I can't think straight right now. I need to take a piss first." I started toward the entrance.

Tockner followed me to the portable toilets on site. I chose the larger one intended for disabled visitors. After taking a quick look to make sure no one was nearby, he joined me inside and closed the door.

Tockner was built fairly well, his torso surprisingly like the one in the photo I'd clipped out of a magazine that I used to post when escorting. His hair was ash, not my favorite color, but his short chest hair lay in an attractive pattern. I loved rubbing my beard against it.

We couldn't take long, though, in case someone walked up and stood outside waiting for their turn. Another moment of rubbing, a moment of kissing, and then two moments to get him off. He left the booth first. I waited for his knock to tell me the coast was clear, and I exited, too.

"One of these days…" he said as we headed back to the parking lot.

"What?"

"I might take you out for dinner."

"O…kay."

"We'll need to butch you up a bit first."

"I used to wear fake facial scars for Halloween when I was a kid."

He laughed. "Maybe you can apply some fake bruises and we'll pretend I'm talking to you about an assault."

Dating a closeted gay cop sounded problematic, even if I wasn't already partnered. I remembered listening to the radio show "Says You," where one of the segments asked contestants the difference between words that seemed to mean the same thing, like "burglary" and "robbery." If only I'd known back in Italy the distinction between "threesome," "throuple," and "triad."

I'd watched, enthralled, one evening while a young gay couple danced to "Sarà Perché Ti Amo" next to the jukebox at the train station in Frascati.

"Have you ever thought about getting a tattoo?" Tockner asked.

"I hate needles."

"Then get one on your back. You won't see the needles."

"But I won't see the tattoo, either." What I really wanted was the image of an earwig on my left earlobe with a single drop of blood. But that might be awkward while working at the bank.

"How about this?" Tockner asked. "Next time we hook up, I'll bring a Sharpie and draw something on your ass."

The suggestion sent a tingle through my groin. "What'll you draw?"

He shook his head. "You'll have to have sex with someone else afterward and ask them."

"Recommending anyone?" I asked.

He waggled his eyebrows, stepped into his car, and drove off.

Laughter was the best medicine, everyone said, but friendly sex wasn't a bad back up. You made do with what you had.

Before walking the last two blocks home, I had to restrain myself from knocking on Elijah's door. He almost certainly knew more about Nick, but I didn't want to use either food or sex to wheedle it out of him.

I kept thinking about what Mr. Gustafson said. There was no reason to believe the custodian was lying, but then, I didn't know him well enough to know what reasons he might have.

The investigation wasn't making me feel better. Perhaps it could have if I was any good at this. But I also remembered watching Salvo Montalbano looking only minimally satisfied at the end of an episode. When all was said and done, a person had still been murdered. There was never going to be any way to be okay with that.

Before the pandemic, I sometimes visited the adult video store in White Center. They had a row of cubicles with glory holes as well as three theaters, two straight and one gay. Rishab, one of the regulars, talked to me sometimes about his depression. I'd told him about an article discussing psychedelics being used to treat the condition, and he brought some mushrooms to share with me on my next visit.

I'd been too scared to ever try them.

I'd kept them hidden in my office at home for two months, trying to work up the nerve. In the end, I was afraid our house would be targeted because Tony and I were gay. Enough conservative homophobes were in the FBI and local law enforcement that I'd be an easy target after protesting against white supremacists. I couldn't take the chance police would find mushrooms in my underwear drawer.

I finally threw the baggie away without ever trying the treatment.

The nearest clinical trial was in San Francisco.

That was also where I'd need to go if I wanted a visa to live abroad.

I couldn't get out of the country and Nick couldn't get back into housing, but we had created a kind of Mutual Aid society to help one another.

And he still needed a bit more help.

Tony and I watched an episode of *Midnight Mass* on Netflix while we ate dinner in silence. After I washed the dishes, I got ready for my visit with Roger and Krichelle and kissed Tony goodbye.

"It's always about what *you* want, isn't it?" he asked. "When are you going to have some time for *me*?"

"Next Thursday is Free First Thursday," I said. "It's my day off. Why don't you take off, too, and we'll do something fun?" Several museums around town waived admission once a month.

"And what if I don't want to use a vacation day just to accommodate your schedule? Not everyone gets to have four-day work weeks."

"Then I'll text you from the museum."

"You're such an asshole, Morgan, and not the good kind."

And he wasn't the good kind of prick, either. But maybe it was best I was too tired to tell him.

***

Krichelle set out a bowl of grapes and a saucer filled with cheese cubes, keeping any chips or cookies she might have hidden in the pantry so as not to tempt me. I brought four cans of lemon seltzer water. Years ago, resisting sugary treats might have been a struggle. But now when I looked at foods I couldn't eat, I was so aware of the consequences that avoiding them felt routine. I wouldn't eat a corn chip any more than I'd lay out shirtless in bright sunlight for five hours.

Valentina wore a sweatshirt reading "See you in hell" in pastel lettering. Krichelle wore pearl-shaped jade earrings.

Roger, even with his slightly pudgy dad bod, wore a T-shirt so tight I could see the edge of each areola.

"Morgan," he said, "my eyes are up here."

Valentina giggled.

We chatted a few minutes about Krichelle's work before getting down to our Scrabble game. Right-wing nutjobs were still blathering about "woke" schools providing litter boxes so that kids identifying as cats could shit in them. Female high school students had to submit detailed reports about their menstrual cycles before they were allowed to play sports.

"Hey, we're here to have fun!" Krichelle said. We each picked out tiles to determine who would go first. Roger won.

He put down B-O-N-E.

"Really, Dad? Four letters?"

He shrugged. Then Krichelle added a D and an E in front of his word.

"Way to go, Mom!"

German words were now considered legal in the game, but it wasn't likely even with a little cheating anyone was going to come up with "buchhandlung" or "Gemeindezentrum."

Krichelle tried to keep the conversation light, steering it back to a safe subject whenever I inevitably mentioned something gloomy. It crossed my mind I might be their version of a Mormon "service project." The idea felt so humiliating I made more of an effort to say something cheery.

It wasn't easy.

"Valentina, have you read any of the *Little House* books?" I'd already brought up *Astrid and Lilly Save the World* and *Enola Holmes*. But after we discussed *Wednesday*, I realized I'd been drifting toward the gloomy again.

"Like *Little House on the Prairie*?" she asked, her brows furrowing.

"I read all of them in college." I put down the word "cove," which Roger amended to "alcove."

"You took a course in *Little House* books?" Valentina asked incredulously.

Krichelle put an N in front of an existing "ova," and then added O-T-E under her N.

"I read them on my own."

"Oh, my god," Valentina said. "Were you out? Could anyone tell you were gay?" She completed the word "zoo" on the board and added her new points happily.

"They couldn't even tell when I was singing 'Dancing Queen' for the school talent show." I thought for a second and added a K and an A in front of Valentina's last word.

"I'm surprised you survived to adulthood," Roger commented.

We continued playing for another thirty minutes, the time between moves growing longer and longer. And because I was so mired in gloomy thoughts, I couldn't help bringing the conversation down again. I caught them up on the latest information I had about Nick's murder.

Only it didn't really feel like we were discussing clues, discussing a case. It didn't even feel like gossiping. I remembered being assigned by my bishop to stake out a member of our congregation suspected of having an affair. I was to follow him if he left the house, as his wife had complained he took an unnaturally long time to run simple errands on the weekend.

Members of the church in Salt Lake and other heavily Mormon areas were sometimes assigned to stake out gay bars and write down the license plates in the area for cross-referencing.

We said things like "gosh darn it!" and "dagnabbit!" and "flip!" Minced oaths, proxy curses while keeping ourselves pure.

Wholesome, clean-shaven narks and double agents.

Perhaps I had more training as a sleuth than I thought.

"When I die," I said, "I want the funeral home to play 'Another One Bites the Dust.'"

That didn't come out nearly as light as I'd intended.

"Not me," Valentina said, shaking her head. "I think when I die, I'm going to have Ouija boards handed out at my funeral. Or maybe crystal balls. Tell everyone to 'keep in touch!'"

Roger threw a grape at her. She caught it in her mouth.

***

Walking home, I decided to bring my *Little House* books the next time I visited. I still possessed them, all these years later. I still had my First Edition copy of *The Secret Garden*, too, from when I collected Victorian books for their beautiful covers. The novel was technically Edwardian, but it *felt* Victorian. I also owned an early French edition of *From the Earth to the Moon*, with its even more exquisite cover. The Duga family was good to me, and it wasn't as if I was going to leave any of this to children of my own.

God only knew if they'd throw it all away two days after inheriting it.

I'd felt guilty even ten and twenty years ago buying these items, such an extravagance when climate organizations needed funds to battle fossil fuel corporations. But beauty felt important even in desperate times.

I'd made a will leaving my half of the house to Tony, but I probably needed to add an addendum, listing Roger and Krichelle as beneficiaries if something happened to Tony and me at the same time.

Evangelical Christians were preaching that vaccines were being used to inject parasitic eggs into people. They claimed that "fake meat" was made of demons, that a portal to hell had opened over the White House the moment Biden took office.

These were the folks calling for Article V so they could rewrite the Constitution. We were only a handful of states away.

It was difficult not to expect to be murdered, even before what happened to Nick.

Perhaps Valentina would live to see the end of capitalism. If I couldn't help "the world," I might at least help her. More mutual aid. There was no one else to turn to except one another.

I could change the beneficiary on my life insurance through the bank without Tony ever knowing. I would have to think about it again on Monday.

I couldn't leave any note, any email, have any conversation that revealed my unhappiness, anything that might give the insurance company a reason to rule my death a suicide and refuse to pay out.

The rear of a pickup truck parked on 61st sported two bumper stickers, and the rear glass window on the cab had a large decal pasted to it. One bumper sticker read, "Let's go Brandon!" and the other "Pro-God, Pro-Gun, Pro-Trump." Right here in liberal Seattle. In a neighborhood that was at most 40% white.

I was afraid to post political signs in our yard. I used to light a menorah in the window during Hanukkah, but I'd stopped that soon after the 2016 election.

The large decal on the pickup's rear window listed a column of figures: .22, .380, 9 mm, .40, and .45. A column beside it read "All faster than dialing 911."

The truck owner wasn't promising to protect the innocent from criminal threat—he promised to *be* the threat from which someone else would need protection. The far right didn't just hate us. They wanted us dead. The only thing keeping them back was fear of personal consequences. Once that was gone, nothing would stop them.

These people believed that Biden was a robot, that Democrats drank the blood of children.

Absurdity wasn't funny. It was dangerous.

The only way late-stage capitalism could survive a little longer was by pitting us against each other. And since capitalism was everywhere, there was really no escaping it. But there were at least degrees of misery, like Dante's levels of hell. And I wanted a better level.

Maybe if I was accepted into the Arctic Circle expedition, I'd stay over in Norway afterward. I'd already started learning the basics. "Hallo." "Hvor mye koster det?" "Vil du ha sex?"

I could always jump overboard in the middle of the night.

Of course, my bypass surgery should be months behind me by then, and I might have found a new hope in the future.

When I reached our house, I paused before climbing the steps. The light was on in Tony's office. I should really say something nice, offer to do something with him in the morning. We both had Saturday off, after all.

Just as I inserted the key in the lock, my cell rang. I looked at the number and frowned before picking up.

"Mr. Beylerian?" a voice asked. "Can we talk?"

It was Harold Gustafson.

Chapter Thirteen: Trash We Leave Behind

I walked down to light rail rather than catch the bus on Saturday morning. Twenty-five minutes of gentle exercise wasn't much, but it was better than doomscrolling. Just fifteen minutes online before leaving the house had revealed that 14,000 people in Tacoma were without power because of late night attacks on four substations. Seven dumpsters had been set on fire overnight in the Central District here in Seattle. Authorities suspected white supremacists in the first instance and homeless people in the second.

The biggest mistake with doomscrolling was trying to engage. After listening to talking heads discuss the effectiveness of throwing a can of tomato soup at the glass shield covering a famous painting, I typed a simple comment: Tone isn't the problem. No one ever solved a global crisis by using a polite tone.

You'd have thought I'd advocated blowing up gas stations. I logged off, committing not to even check again for at least two days.

Disengaging felt cowardly but engaging with closed minds was useless as well as disheartening. And disheartening opponents was their goal.

A tall, pear-shaped black man with unusually large lips boarded light rail at Othello, the seat of his sweatpants damp with a yellowish-brown liquid. His vacant look made me wonder whether he was intellectually disabled or simply stoned.

I remembered hearing someone once ask an anthropologist the earliest sign of civilization. "It's when I find a human bone that has healed," she said. "That means the injured person wasn't left to die but was taken care of until they recovered."

Light rail continued zipping northward toward downtown. Mr. Gustafson had promised to let me into the offices while he did his weekend custodial work. I brought along some nitrile gloves so as not to leave fingerprints, but that seemed just as incriminating as my presence if I was caught. While I didn't feel bright enough to recognize anything relevant if I saw it, there seemed few options for pursuing justice other than blindly poking about.

"No one's due in today," Mr. Gustafson said when he opened the door. "Take a look around. I won't be far away if you need me." He was only responsible for just the one floor.

"I'll start with the offices." No cubicle worker would be in a position to sign the contract that had gotten Nick into trouble.

"I've unlocked all of them."

I looked up into a corner near the ceiling.

"No security cameras."

That made sense, I supposed, or Nick would already have been able to clear his name. Unless the guilty party had erased the footage. I headed for the nearest office but still looked about furtively for cameras inside. Mr. Gustafson could be lying, after all. This could all be a set up.

Nothing interesting in the trash in the first two offices. I glanced carefully through the contents of several desk drawers but saw nothing that screamed murderer. The results were the same in the third office, and the fourth.

The fifth office belonged to Mr. Marklund. I made sure not to move anything without replacing it exactly where it had been before. But there was nothing of interest here, either. Most files these days were digital, and I wasn't about to try logging onto anyone's computer. Every workplace required passwords, often a different one for each application employees accessed.

I felt like Gaëlle in *Perfect Murders*, a traffic cop accidentally brought into a murder investigation and learning on the job.

Only I wasn't learning anything.

It was time to take a break, so I headed to the employee bathroom on the far side of the cubicles. The combination of age and diabetes meant I could never go more than a couple of hours without peeing. And when the urge hit, it hit hard and fast.

Some drugs, like metformin, might not even be able to work if we didn't have the right gut microbiome to metabolize it into its active form.

I rushed into the bathroom and unzipped quickly, though my stream was as weak as ever. The last few drops were slowly dripping out when the door opened behind me.

Mr. Gustafson hadn't invited me down here as a sexual ruse, had he? I'd gotten no gay vibes, and he was good-looking enough he could easily do better.

"Mr...Mr...Baylor?"

I whipped around, flinging one last drop of urine onto the floor. Elodie gasped and jumped back while I quickly zipped up. "Miss Bliquez," I said. "How are you?" I wasn't about to correct her understanding of my name.

"Wh-what are you doing here?"

"I, uh, I hit it off with Harold the other day and invited him to lunch. He asked me to meet him at work."

"Oh."

"I hope that wasn't inappropriate," I said, shrugging guiltily. "I'm afraid I kind of insisted. I mean, what can I say?" I shrugged again. "He's hot and I get to watch him bend over a lot."

Mr. Gustafson joined Elodie in the bathroom doorway, his eyes wide. I wasn't sure how much he'd heard. "Sweetie," I said, "I think Miss Bliquez will probably want me to wait downstairs."

The next three seconds seemed to last an eternity.

I remembered the mirrors in the temple sealing room.

"Oh," Elodie said nervously, "I suppose it's okay. Just don't...don't..." She tried to peer into the bathroom trash without moving closer to it.

"We won't have sex here," I assured her.

Mr. Gustafson blinked a couple of times. "Is...there something you need today, Miss?"

She shook her head. "No. I think I lost my earrings somewhere."

"Not those lovely dragonflies!" I exclaimed.

Elodie gave a shy smile which faded quickly. "I bought some new ones," she said. "Erik—Mr. Marklund—likes skiing. So these were two sets of dangly skis."

"I'm gonna get back to work." Mr. Gustafson walked off, leaving Elodie and me alone in the bathroom. I pointed toward the cubicles behind her and we both exited the intimate space. She absentmindedly led us toward the reception desk.

"Poor Harold," she said. "He and Mr. Degraff always got along so well."

"How did everyone react back when Mr. Degraff...caused all that trouble?" Best to make that question as open ended as possible.

"I didn't believe it at first," she said. She looked off toward the bathroom. "But you never really know what people are like on the inside."

I couldn't think of a good follow-up question. Even Inspector Coliandro could do a better job.

"And you lost the earrings here?" I asked. Brilliant.

"Mr. Marklund had me take them off when..." We reached her desk. "Yes, I lost them at work."

Elodie didn't seem to want to check her boyfriend's office or any of the trash bins. She just sat at her desk looking a bit melancholy. Marklund probably hadn't said anything nice about the new earrings, almost certainly finding them problematic in some way.

"How long have you known Mr. Marklund?" I asked, trying to make conversation. I was hardly the person to provide relationship advice, but there was no reason not to try alleviating at least a little of her pain while she was here. Once the receptionist left, I might be able to resume my snooping.

"Two years," she said. "He's the one who got me this job." She frowned when she said it and I wondered how trapped she felt.

"That was nice of him," I told her, feeling like an idiot. Small talk as a missionary had been excruciating. *"Fa bel tempo oggi, no? Vuoi leggere il Libro di Mormon?"*

"Do you suppose," Elodie said slowly, "if I have a baby, it makes up for...?" Her voice trailed off.

For killing someone, I wanted to ask? I felt a shiver and rubbed my arms. The young woman might have finished her question in a dozen other ways, but it was impossible not to hear that conclusion first.

"Net zero?" I asked.

She stared at the floor and nodded.

Jesus Christ in a camper. What the fuck had just happened here?

Marklund or someone else at Nick's workplace might very well be the killer, but the truth was I'd never know. Detectives needed search warrants to find evidence and even then often failed to come up with any. I could be looking right at a murderer and never discover anything which might prove useful in a court of law.

This was detective masturbation. And it wasn't nearly as innocuous as mental masturbation.

Elodie continued staring at the floor in silence.

I tried to say something supportive but it sounded insincere even to my own ears. "Don't wait until you're my age to live the life you want," I said. Trite, but what else could I offer? "Making a change only gets harder as you grow older."

I'd dropped out of nursing school when my partner at the time grew impatient with the long hours required for study. I'd known even then the relationship wouldn't last and assumed I'd go back to school after we broke up, but somehow, I never did, flitting about from one low-paying job to another, afraid to take on such an overwhelming project again.

And one year led to the next and the next and…

If I retired next year at sixty-two, my monthly Social Security check would be just over $929. Even if I waited until I was sixty-five, the amount would only rise another hundred and fifty dollars. If I managed to work until I was sixty-seven, I still wouldn't receive enough to live on. Not even if I worked five full days a week at my current wage. Or six days. Or seven.

And if I didn't lose this weight, I wouldn't live anywhere near long enough to retire regardless of the amount.

I heard the word "crabs" and remembered Elodie was still talking. "Excuse me?" So much for being supportive.

The young woman blushed. "I don't know why I'm telling you all this."

I did. She had no one else. Her boyfriend had probably already cut her off from her usual friends. And I'd always had a certain air about me. Even after I'd been excommunicated, coworkers at various jobs had routinely confided in me. One of them told me, "You kind of seem like a priest."

"So he's not faithful?" I asked.

"He never said he would be," she admitted. "I just thought…"

"Hard to look for another job, isn't it, when the other employer needs to check in with HR?"

Elodie stood. "I'd better get back home. He gets worried if I'm gone too long."

"Elodie," I said softly, "if—"

"I found them!" Mr. Gustafson waved from the bathroom door. "They were in the trash." He waved silver earrings in the air.

Elodie rushed over to grab them, hugging the jewelry to her chest.

"You should disinfect those before you put them back in your ears." The custodian's eyes met mine. He probably wouldn't have thought to check the bathroom trash bags if Elodie hadn't shown up today.

She gave him a kiss on the cheek and hurried out of the office with a last, happy wave. I turned to Mr. Gustafson.

"The signatures were in Mr. Degraff's trash can," he said. "It's why I didn't think much about them until after."

"Which was his office?"

He pointed to the fourth room I'd searched.

"I've already started looking for another job."

"I think that's wise."

Mr. Marklund was an ass, but he wasn't the boss. Still, the atmosphere in the office felt less than healthy. While there were some unsavory characters here, it really wasn't likely anyone at the company had direct involvement in Nick's death. The simplest explanation was that the man was robbed, and the simplest answer was usually right. The guilt Nick's coworkers shared lay in putting him in a physically vulnerable position to begin with.

I needed to visit Nick's ward in north Seattle on Sunday to see if the guilty party showed up there. That was also unlikely, but there was no point in not seeing this through. "Don't stop just short of the Celestial Kingdom,"

I'd heard every week in church. I groaned thinking about my commute in the morning.

"You okay?"

I nodded.

Mr. Gustafson turned back to the bathroom, putting a new trash can liner in the metal bin that slid out from the wall. He stared into it a moment before pushing it back in place. "I know you were just making up a cover story," he said.

"Um…"

"About us going out."

"Yeah."

"I'm not gay."

I was trying to come up with a clever remark when he continued. "But I did take a shower this morning."

Perhaps I should have felt put upon, pressured. Taken for granted maybe. But I didn't feel any of that, or gratitude, either. I simply gave off "my hole is your hole" vibes. It was what it was.

There were worse vibes in the world.

I sat on the toilet and opened my mouth. Woody Guthrie could have written a song about me.

Mr. Gustafson had used a lavender-scented soap that morning. Quite thoughtful of him.

Chapter Fourteen: Trash We Carry with Us

I knew I was overreacting. Or acting out. Or being self-destructive. Being an idiot. Whatever it was, it wasn't healthy.

Petula Clark had stopped Karen Carpenter in their dressing room once before a performance and told her, "I don't know what you're doing, but stop it!"

I boarded light rail at Pioneer Square after leaving Nick's workplace and immediately caught the attention of a slim, forty-something Asian man who invited me to his place on Beacon Hill by using his eyes alone.

Perhaps Hulu could do a limited series based on my life. *Stories of a Sleazy Sleuth.*

But fat people were only appealing if they were funny.

Tony and I had chosen an open relationship from the start. Neither of us had been especially promiscuous, only spending time with other men four or five times a year. That had increased slightly as the years passed, but it was the pandemic that reset our behavior. Forced into absolute monogamy for two years, we'd just started experimenting with sexual excursions again when monkeypox hit the community. Even self-imposed lockdowns took an emotional toll. Two additional vaccinations later and we both pretty much threw caution to the wind.

I might not want someone to breathe on me, but I couldn't get enough cum.

When Tony and I had first moved in together, we kissed each other in every doorway of the house. Over the next few weeks, we had sex in every room.

He could barely look at me now.

I remembered the teenage boys in Cagliari who'd spit on me and kicked my companion. The car that had chased us down a country road outside Ciampino and sprayed mud on us.

The woman who'd thrown a bucket of water from her balcony as we pushed buttons on her building's citofono.

I also remembered the night of the earthquake when our roof collapsed during a baptismal service in Salerno and I'd been separated from the other elders in the chaos. An older man had huddled with me on the beach all night to keep me warm.

The Asian man led me to his bedroom, slipped on a condom, and fucked me for ten minutes. He never removed his mask, kicking me out after his orgasm with another silent look.

On the elevator back down to the Beacon Hill platform, I tried propositioning another man with my eyes. He looked at my stomach and rolled his own eyes in response.

Karen Carpenter had felt fat even as she starved herself to death.

But I was Mama Cass.

I stood in the bike section of the train car and held onto a hook as the doors closed. After quickly scanning for possible shooters, I relaxed until the next stop. I was going to do something fun the rest of the day, forget about Nick, move on with my life. I would read a Marshall Thornton novel, watch a Belgian science fiction show about disappearing people, listen to some feel-good music on Pandora.

Perhaps "Sugar, Sugar" by the Archies.

I squeezed my eyes shut and tried to block out the world but there were cracks in every shell I could muster.

A rail-thin white man, tattooed and wearing dirty clothes, boarded the train, walking back and forth across the car, pausing at empty seats but not sitting, then pausing next to seated riders and moving on again. Passengers kept track of his movements out of the corner of their eyes.

When the man approached me, I moved to make room in the bike rack area and nodded. He paused, waving his arms theatrically, and kept walking.

Was I having a nervous breakdown?

I remembered a documentary about a terrorist attack in Paris, where dozens of concertgoers were killed at the Bataclan. Several people had hidden in a bathroom upstairs. Afraid the terrorists were heading their way, they decided to climb up into the false ceiling.

One woman recounted how she tried to encourage everyone else to go ahead of her. She was too fat. She'd slow everyone down. They insisted, though, and she tried.

She broke the lid on the toilet. She was terrified of dying and almost as terrified of being scolded for her weight. But the others, strangers also afraid of dying, wouldn't give up. They pulled from above and pushed from below and got that woman to safety. Then the others still in the bathroom below followed as quickly as they could.

They were so well hidden they were the last to be discovered by the police.

***

"Out fucking around again?" Tony asked when I walked back into the house.

"Only twice," I said.

He scoffed in disgust. "Meanwhile, my e-bike was stolen."

"I'm sorry," I said. But why did he make that sound like my fault?

"If you didn't encourage all these homeless people to hang around…"

Ah.

"Do you want to go buy another one?" I asked. Tony didn't believe in insurance, which was why I paid the homeowner's insurance by myself. "I can help with a hundred dollars."

"Don't bother." He turned and headed to his office at the rear of the house. "You'll need that to feed your *friends.*"

As it turned out, I didn't read a book or watch TV or listen to music. I sat on the front porch and watched two hummingbirds fight at the feeder all afternoon.

How in the world did they have enough energy to spare?

I prepared dinner later, an Impossible burger and macaroni salad for Tony and some fermented foods for me. Since gut microbiome influenced weight gain and depression and all sorts of things, I'd bought some kombucha tea, refrigerated sauerkraut, refrigerated pickles, cottage cheese with active cultures, and some tempeh. Just a bit of each, especially since some of it wasn't very good, and I was done.

Perhaps if I ate like this *every* day and not just once a week…

After dinner, we watched another episode of *Midnight Mass* and then a gay German movie called *100 Things*. Tony mostly texted with friends while I read the subtitles. But at least he hadn't left the room.

Maybe I wasn't mourning Nick so much as the death of my marriage. I was nothing if not self-aware.

A few years back, Tony and I had argued about subconscious motivations. "I don't have any subconscious motivations," he'd told me.

On the screen in front of me, Paul and his best friend were about halfway through their quest. I clicked the Pause button. "Wanna have sex?" I asked.

Tony turned to me. "Do you have cooties?"

"Do you?"

Tony grunted and finished the text he was working on. I was just about to unpause the movie when he put his phone down. "We'll have to turn out the light," he said. "I can't get hard if I see you."

I turned off the television while he turned off the lamp. I heard the rustle of clothes and expected to find Tony's dick in my face but instead realized he'd shoved his ass in my direction. I pried his cheeks open and licked away while he jacked off. A few minutes later, he grunted again as he came.

"Stand up," he ordered, "and pull down your pants."

I felt a hand pasting something warm and sticky in my ass crack.

"Now pull your pants up."

I did so while he turned the lights back on.

"How about an episode of *Worst Roommate Ever?*" he suggested, picking up the remote.

Un-fucking-believable.

I remembered the day my companion in Napoli threatened to kill me. And I suddenly understood why no police department in the world could ever have enough detectives to do their job successfully.

***

I woke up early the next morning, vowing to take a day off from doomscrolling but unable to keep myself from clicking on a headline about a right-wing governor banning Black Studies courses in his state. I clicked out of the news, opened a Word doc, and wrote some notes for an op-ed. "Don't Say Gay. Don't Say Black. Don't Say Equality. Don't Say Human Rights. But Do, Please, Say God." An awfully long title, and I just couldn't pull together my ideas into anything coherent enough to submit.

People aged when their telomeres grew shorter. But souls withered and died, too, when bombarded non-stop with toxic behavior.

It *had* to be okay to take a step back.

I pulled on my nicest slacks and best polo shirt and headed north. There was still a bit of dried cum on my ass, but that felt appropriate for the occasion. Looking for Nick's killer at church was a waste of time, of course, but the alternative of spending the day at home with Tony felt even more futile.

The ward meetinghouse was old, probably built in the 1940's, and so had a bit of character, nothing like the cookie cutter chapels built over the past few decades. In my day, Priesthood meeting had been first, divided into the Elders Quorum for younger men and the High Priests Group for older men, whether or not those older men had received higher callings. They still needed to feel superior in some way. These days, all the adult men met together, and it looked like Priesthood meeting would take place after Sacrament.

It also appeared there was no more Sunday School. A pity, as Gospel Doctrine had been the only remotely interesting part of Sunday services before.

I'd only seen a photo of Amanda once but didn't recognize her mingling about. One young man, a recent RM probably, came over to ask if I was investigating the church. My lack of suit and tie gave me away.

"Um, yes," I said.

"How did you hear about us?" He looked around for the local missionaries.

"I worked with Nick Degraff," I said.

The young man frowned, but I couldn't tell if he simply didn't recognize the name. Given the age difference, they weren't likely to have been friends.

"I was upset when he was fired," I continued. "I know he was a man of God."

"Yes, yes," the young man said quickly. "Let me go find some elders for you."

Soon I was saddled with two young missionaries who sat on either side of me during Sacrament meeting. If they'd sat a little closer, perhaps the meeting would have been more interesting. As it was, all I could think about was how to approach some of the older men later.

I refused to eat a piece of the squished bread that was passed about the chapel, pinched off a loaf by teenage boys who probably hadn't washed their hands since the night before.

Not that I hadn't put filthier things in my mouth lately.

The talks during Sacrament meeting were as superficial and unresearched as I remembered. A teen who'd never worked a day in his life spoke on the importance of tithing, followed by a young single adult woman who spoke on the importance of families.

I should bring Elijah a Sunday pastry on my way home.

I studied the faces of the bishop and his counselors on the stand, glanced around the chapel at the faces of fathers and mothers trying to keep their kids quiet enough not to embarrass them. I'd watched *Under the Banner of Heaven*, but this congregation didn't look especially threatening.

Killers from Kolob might make a fun movie, perhaps an instant classic like *Attack of the Killer Tomatoes*.

I wondered if Tony was planning to find another partner and spring it on me without warning.

I wondered if I'd mind.

The second counselor in the bishopric stood up and began the last talk of the service, delivering his words in that droning, monotonous tone indistinguishable from that of any apostle or seventy I'd ever heard during General Conference.

These folks were more boring than I was, and that was saying something.

"We do these things to please Heavenly Father," the second counselor continued, though I hadn't been following closely enough to remember his latest points.

"We do these things so we can be with our families throughout eternity."

Unless you got a temple divorce, I reflected.

Mormons had moved away from open discussion of becoming gods in the afterlife, but it was all we'd talked about when I was growing up. I remembered how shocked I'd felt when Elder Fackler, one of my junior companions, told me the only reason he was serving a mission was because his father had promised to buy him a car. "Aren't you being sort of a puttana?" I'd asked him. I wasn't trying to put him down. It was an honest question.

"And why are *you* here?" Elder Fackler had asked in return.

"To serve God," I'd said.

"Why?" my companion pressed.

"Well, because…because…"

"Because it'll help you get to the Celestial Kingdom?"

"Um…"

"Isn't the Celestial Kingdom a reward?" he asked. "A payout?"

"Um…"

"Capisco," Elder Fackler had replied. "Capisco completamente."

So I'd been less shocked later when I learned another companion had earned the money for his mission by loan sharking at Brigham Young, when I learned one of the district leaders had earned money for his two years by selling drugs in Orem.

When had I stopped living in the present, I asked myself, looking toward the podium. I seemed to compare everything I did these days to something I'd seen, heard, or done in the past. I was a Walking Memoir.

The words to the Cranberries' "Zombie" flashed through my brain.

Derry Girls was such a great show.

"So I asked him," the second counselor droned on, "why he was bothering to throw starfish into the ocean. There were too many on the beach to save and the sun was too hot. Almost all of them were going to die. 'Are you even making a difference?' I asked him.

"And I remember what he said next." The second counselor made a dramatic pause and lifted his hand as if holding something invisible. "He said, 'It makes a difference to this one' and he threw it back in the ocean. 'It makes a difference to this one.'"

Chapter Fifteen: Treasures We Cling To

"Are you planning to move in?" Elijah opened his camper door and ushered me inside.

I handed him the piece of key lime pie I'd bought at Safeway. None of the older men in Priesthood meeting had been willing to talk to me about Nick. I'd learned nothing at all from my morning excursion.

Maybe I could come up with at least one good question for Elijah.

His eyes narrowed. "It's not that I don't appreciate all this," he said, "but you're getting to be a little clingy."

Ouch.

"If your life is so messed up you need to hang out with me, you probably need to think about fixing yourself."

"I just—"

Elijah put his hand on my shoulder. "I'm never getting out of this camper, Morgan."

"Don't say that. You—"

"My soul is too tired."

But that was why I was here, I wanted to tell him, to ease his burden, to give him hope, to…

"I got nothing for you today," he said.

I nodded and stepped out of the camper. The realization that I was dragging him down was too mortifying to contemplate.

If I could only find the murderer, perhaps I could provoke him to slit my throat, too.

I gritted my teeth. This pity party needed to end a long time ago.

Before heading the rest of the way up the hill, I looked at Nick's camper one more time. It still hadn't been towed. Perhaps it was only a matter of time before someone else started squatting. It was certainly serving no purpose empty.

Despite the housing shortage, at last count over sixteen million homes in the U.S. were considered vacant. The shortage was because people couldn't afford to live in them.

Folks had moved into a half burned out fast food restaurant on Rainier six months ago.

I stared at the dirty white walls of Nick's camper and tried to will them to speak.

Perhaps I should make some kind of public announcement that I knew who the killer was and wait for him to come after me while I napped on the sofa. If there were never enough evidence to convict the man for Nick's murder, the police might be able to convict him for mine.

Selling my house and divvying up the property seemed overwhelming. Tony was petty and spiteful. I didn't have the energy to face it all.

Maybe *I'd* come sleep in Nick's camper tonight. It had almost started feeling more like home than my own house, anyway.

Spending time with Nick had been fun. Reminiscing about our missionary days. I'd teased him by singing "I Think I Love You" with my best David Cassidy impression and he'd teased me by singing "I'm Too Sexy" in a gravelly voice. He talked about what life might be like in the Millennium, and I talked about socialism, simply calling it the Millennium, too, so he'd listen without feeling nervous.

One week he'd be hopeful, in despair the next, and hopeful again on my next visit. If I could have just kept visiting…

Nick had once shown me a photo of some custom keycaps for the keyboard on his home computer. Lots of different dog breeds. I thought it might be fun to customize my personal keyboard as well, replace the M with an image of a Maiasaura, replace the O with an image of an

Oviraptor, replace the T with an image of a Tyrannosaurus rex, and so forth. I'd use a Dimetrodon for the D, even if it wasn't technically a dinosaur but a synapsid like humans.

I'd have no trouble recognizing which letters were being represented. I did take a dinosaur course in college, after all.

But those keycaps could cost $16 apiece or more. I'd need far more disposable income to justify an extravagance like that.

I did still think it was important to treat myself once in a while. Donating every spare dollar, every spare minute, to even the most important social justice issues wasn't sustainable without having a little fun once in a while.

When Nick offered to fuck me on my fourth visit, I didn't say no.

Rodgers and Hammerstein lyrics floated through my head.

Tony accused me of taking advantage of homeless folks. And I wasn't sure he was wrong. Sexually, it was usually fun, and pretending there was a remote possibility I was lightening their load—ha!—was even more rewarding.

But money was power, and I had more money than they did. So there was a built-in power difference in our relationship. Even if Nick thought he was offering himself willingly, he might subconsciously feel he couldn't say no after once saying yes. I might still be guilty of statutory manipulation.

Just a couple of weeks ago, Nick said he'd have made a bad gay man, that he'd feel far too vulnerable to let another man inside him.

"Why?" I'd asked.

"Because…it might be nasty back there."

"Gay men do take showers," I pointed out. I'd explained douching as well. And he seemed willing enough to fuck me that day. But first, I asked him to lie on his stomach after undressing. I promised not to penetrate him and in fact remained clothed. I leaned over, pulled his cheeks apart, and rimmed him.

"Oh, I'm embarrassed!" he whispered. Even a lot of gay guys got freaked out, both on the giving and receiving end. But it wasn't as if people stopped knowing how to bathe the moment they became homeless. I routinely bought baby wipes and toilet paper for Nick.

"That's okay," I assured him and kept up what I'd started. Nick finally relaxed and let me continue for another twenty minutes.

When I finished, he sat up and looked at me for a long moment. "Amanda would never do that," he said. "And I don't think I'd want her to. But I've never felt physically closer to anyone before."

"If you get back together, you might look into pegging." He frowned, and I explained.

You could feel close to someone without having sex, of course, without even being attracted to them.

"Everything happens for a reason," he said softly. Ridiculous, of course, but I wasn't going to deny him the right to make his misery meaningful. I kept a notecard posted next to my PC at home with the words "Happiness isn't the goal. Lead a meaningful life."

If Nick couldn't get his former life back, I'd at least wanted his new life to be bearable.

I handed Nick his shirt, but he shook his head, pulling mine up over my head instead. "I think fucking you will feel a little different for me this time." And in fact, though I knew Nick wasn't even bisexual, it almost felt like lovemaking.

Perhaps I was every bit as delusional as right-wing Christians who believed JFK, Jr. was still alive and palling around with insurrectionists.

I'd never get to sing "Someone Left the Cake Out in the Rain" to Nick again.

I was just about to start walking up the hill when something about the camper's license plate caught my eye. A tiny sliver of dirt had been wiped away on one edge. A dog had probably pissed there. I stooped down and cautiously felt behind the plate.

Something was attached on the back. A plastic bag. I tugged on it, and a moment later, I held a freezer bag with folded papers in my hand. "Porca la miseria," I said aloud. I pried open the seal, pulled out the papers, and unfolded them. Finally, I thought, evidence. Playing detective *did* matter.

The writing looked like a password for some type of cryptocurrency account, along with regular bank accounts in his kids' names. "If I only knew how to send ransomware to my old company," Nick had once joked, "I'd make sure my kids were taken care of, no matter what happened to me."

Whatever these papers meant, they were at least something tangible I could hand to the police.

I called the number Klimczyk had given me while I walked up the hill, explaining what I'd found.

"Don't handle it any more than you already have," he ordered. "We'll be over in a few minutes."

Only then did I think about fingerprints. Detective Roche would be so disappointed. I waited on the front porch, setting the bag on the empty chair Tony never used. A car pulled up only moments after I sat down in the matching chair.

"Mr. Beylerian," Detective Stalder said, "you do know that tampering with evidence is a gross misdemeanor, right?"

"It wasn't evidence until I read what was in the bag," I pointed out. "It may still not be."

He walked up the steps and reached for the bag with a gloved hand.

"Nick never mentioned having any money left," I said, "so I don't know if this reflects his finances from a week ago or two years back."

"We'll check it out," Detective Klimczyk assured me.

I debated mentioning Mr. Marklund and the things Elodie and Mr. Gustafson had said. If I didn't tell them and it turned out I should have, I'd look suspicious. If I did and my worries were unfounded, I'd look foolish and perhaps a bit unhinged.

"Keep away from that camper and let us do our job." Stalder practically sneered while Klimczyk closed his eyes and shook his head ever so slightly.

I knew they were playing good cop/bad cop, but did they have to be so cartoonish about it?

"I promise not to sleep in Nick's camper tonight," I said, raising my hand in the scout salute. "At least not in the nude."

Stalder's mouth fell open. Klimczyk had to turn away to keep from laughing.

Chapter Sixteen: Moderation in Excess

"What the hell was that all about?" Tony demanded when I went inside. He'd been listening at the door.

I explained the latest news and then he stormed off to the kitchen. "If you get me in trouble, Morgan, I'll sue your ass."

One of the regulars at the bank was a realtor.

"Your deep concern over your welfare is touching."

Tony spun around and glared. "We have to talk," he said. Then he grabbed his wallet and keys and walked out the door.

I turned on Pandora, listening to Kelly Clarkson and Leona Lewis while I baked some okra and ate two cups of my homemade chicken soup, with my pre-chopped celery, onion, and bok choy, along with some carrots, green beans, water chestnuts, bell peppers, chicken gravy, and canned chicken. My secret ingredient was parmesan cheese. This was my last serving, and I was too tired to make a new batch. It would have to wait until my next day off.

I watched another episode of *Tatort: Streets of Berlin*, one filmed just last year, so most of the characters wore COVID masks at least some of the time. Partitions had been set up between desks in the police station. Everything was matter-of-fact. People adjusted even to global tragedy rather quickly when they had to.

Tonight's episode was about landlords taking advantage of renters.

Late-stage capitalism was the emperor's new clothes.

It was still early, so I rewatched a couple of episodes of *Schitt's Creek*. I loved the one where Patrick sings to David in their store.

Perhaps I should try writing a screenplay. *The Thrilling Adventures of a Couch Potato.*

It looked like Tony wasn't coming back tonight. I beat off onto a T-shirt I hoped to wear someday to a bear party and then sat at my computer, pulling up a playlist of my favorite music videos. "Una sporca poesia," "Una notte che vola via," "Romantici," and "Biancaneve."

While I was partial to San Remo of 1982—I'd watched it on TV with a family we were teaching in northeast Rome—I liked far more than that.

Whenever I listened to Gigliola Cinquetti sing her 1964 Eurovision-winning song, "Non ho l'età," I didn't resent the fact that it was her privilege that allowed her the win. Growing up in a wealthy family, with the opportunity to study piano and music theory, the experience of mingling with sophisticated and connected people even as a teen, she still had to put in the time and effort, still had to exercise some innate talent, to achieve what she did. She did what any of us in the same position would do—followed her dreams. The only thing I resented were the people who wanted to restrict those opportunities to a select few instead of sharing them with, if not everyone, then at least far more than those able to enjoy them now.

I'd spent my teens hoping to become an actor, but I'd been too embarrassed to try, other than singing a couple of duets in our stake's production of *Saturday's Warrior*. And singing Helen Reddy's "I Am Woman" in the youth talent show, substituting the word "Mormon" for "woman."

My father made it clear he wouldn't help me with tuition unless I studied something "useful." And useful subjects left little time for college theater.

Even now, I just wanted enough time and money to join a goddamn gym. Hire a trainer or cook.

I needed $14,000 a year to cover high-dose semaglutide, which my insurance wouldn't cover, despite the financial benefits to them. If I could lose weight, they wouldn't have to cover all the complications from obesity and diabetes and bariatric surgeries.

We needed a presidential emergency order to ramp up production, the way we pushed companies to work on vaccines, the way we ordered production of war supplies during conflicts. Obesity was killing hundreds of thousands of Americans every year, year after year, far greater overall than the number of people killed even during a devastating three-year COVID pandemic.

Was it fair for me to complain about not receiving a $14,000-a-year medication when folks like Nick and Elijah couldn't even get housing?

Yes, I thought it was. We all had the right to demand what we needed to survive.

What I needed now was a windfall of $14,000.

Anyone? Anyone?

I hated Ben Stein's politics.

I hated Nancy Pelosi's politics, too, though I still couldn't fathom how crazy someone had to be to break into her home and attack her husband with a hammer.

I wrote an op-ed on universal healthcare, edited it, edited it again, proofed it, and sent it off to the *Seattle Times.*

When Tony wasn't home, I could imagine living again. I should take the hint.

***

I limited myself to five minutes of doomscrolling Monday morning, enough to learn about a pedestrian bridge collapse in India, a bill in Missouri to ban women in the legislature from showing bare arms, and a gay bar in White Center a block down from the adult video store being set on fire after it closed for the night. Then I listened to Josh Groban's "February Song" and Laura Pausini's "Io sí," and I was ready to face the day.

It helped that I didn't have to say goodbye to Tony.

About halfway to work, a black man without a mask boarded, a former regular at the bank who I hadn't seen in years, maybe a decade.

"Travis?" I asked. "Is that you?"

Travis paused at my seat and then smiled. "Morgan?" he asked. Not bad, considering how long it had been and the fact that my face was half covered.

I nodded. "You still traveling the world?" If I remembered correctly, Travis worked as a home health aide while living in a studio apartment, saving all his money for travel.

His eyes lit up. "Just got back from Uruguay."

I shook my head. "I'm impressed." I paused while he laughed. "Hey, you're living your life," I said. "That's a great thing."

"Well, I didn't buy the last plane ticket, you know."

Elder Fackler had once complained after an elderly man kept us in his apartment for an hour talking about his adventures in North Africa during World War II. "I'm not going to be like him," my companion swore. "Some RM's talk about their missions for the rest of their lives like it was the only interesting thing they ever did." He shook his head. "I'm going to *keep* doing interesting things," he said. "*More* interesting things. I'm not going to be one of those people who keeps an old photo of Reagan on his wall for the rest of my life."

The elderly man who'd droned on had a photo of Mussolini hanging in his living room. At the time, I didn't even know who the guy was.

I hoped, hoped, hoped I was accepted for the Arctic Circle expedition.

Travis continued down the aisle, and an elderly Asian woman with her mask below her nose sat next to me.

The morning passed quickly at the bank, mostly because Joshua was in meetings and unable to pester us. Mr. Easton came to withdraw another $40, a woman came in with a stale-dated check, and I referred another woman to Shanifer for a car loan.

During a brief lull between customers, I looked up the realtor's info on the computer. I wasn't sure I could really make the call, but I wanted that contact number ready the second I decided. I couldn't afford to pay the mortgage by myself for more than one month.

Then, just before lunch, Detectives Stalder and Klimczyk walked into the bank, heading directly to my window, waiting until I finished a transaction and then

Johnny Townsend

taking a last step to the counter. "We need to ask you some questions about Elodie Bliquez," Stalder said.

They couldn't possibly suspect Elodie, could they? Yet they hadn't asked about Mr. Marklund. "Did she accuse someone?" I asked, my brows furrowing. "Did Erik hit her?"

Stalder gave Klimczyk a look. "You seem to know these folks rather well."

"I wanted to see if anyone at Nick's workplace had a motive."

"Mr. Beylerian," Detective Klimczyk said quietly, "is there someplace we can talk?"

178

Chapter Seventeen: Loading the Chamber

The break room was the only option, and I had to ask three employees to step out when we entered. "What's going on?" I asked. "Elodie's okay, isn't she?"

"Why do you say that?"

"You'd hardly be here to tell me she got engaged."

Detective Stalder's eyes narrowed. "Elodie Bliquez was murdered last night."

I sank into a chair at one of the lunch tables.

"But you already knew that, didn't you?"

I looked up at Stalder. "Excuse me?"

"The custodian, Mr. Gustafson, said he saw you two arguing."

What the hell? I opened my mouth to say something but then realized the detective could be lying just to judge my reaction. Masantonio told a witness his partner Riva was called "the macellaio" and would cut off the guy's fingers if he didn't talk.

Orthodox Jews didn't allow butchers to serve on juries.

"Mr. Gustafson did *not* say that," I told the detectives. "If he did, he's embarrassed he asked me to suck his dick. He may be trying to discredit me preemptively."

Stalder snorted. "Mr. Gustafson is married with kids. You telling me you're so irresistible you can turn straight men gay?" He snorted again.

When I was eight, my father had forced me to watch him kill a hog on my grandparents' farm. He'd shot it in the head, but the hog didn't die right away, squealing horrifically for what seemed an eternity. My dad then ran up to the poor creature and stabbed it in the heart.

He forced me to watch him butcher it. When I swore I'd never eat bacon again, my mom asked what difference it made to see the hog die. Every package of store-bought bacon came from a killed hog, too.

Two weeks later, we went on a family outing to a slaughterhouse.

"You asking for a demonstration?" I shifted in my chair to face the cops directly, spreading my legs slightly.

Stalder scowled and took a step forward, stopping when his partner put a hand on his arm.

"Why would I kill Elodie?" I asked. "Because she wouldn't let me suck *her* dick?" I saw the young woman's face, her slumped shoulders. "She just wanted to find her earrings," I said. "Her boyfriend threw them away."

I then recounted the details I could remember from both visits to Nick's workplace, emphasizing the potential forgery. My theories and suspicions all sounded weak and nebulous. Desperate, even.

"Mr. Gustafson didn't say anything about forged signatures," Detective Klimczyk said softly.

"He might be at risk, too," I said. "You might need to watch his back." Damn. I couldn't even remember what that was called. Assigning a bodyguard? That didn't sound right. Staking out his home?

I was such an amateur.

"Any other blow jobs we should know about?" Stalder asked.

I jumped to my feet, feeling a sudden rage it was too late to hide. After an arsonist had killed thirty-two people at a French Quarter gay bar, one of the investigating officers had questioned a suspect, choosing to ask about the man's sex life. "Which one of you is the man?"

The suspect had replied in what I hoped was a surly tone, "Fifty-fifty proposition."

As if asking such a prurient question could possibly help in any way with finding the arsonist.

I looked at my wristwatch. "How much time do you guys have?"

Stalder looked at me a long moment before replying. "No more questions for now," he said. "But Mr. Beylerian?"

"Yes?"

"You should probably get some counseling."

"You paying for it?" I asked.

The detectives walked out of the break room, and I realized my left hand was trembling, my knees wobbly. I sat back down. God damn fucking hell.

Maybe I *should* incriminate myself, I thought, and then plead insanity. It might be the only way to get the mental healthcare I obviously did need.

The door to the break room opened and Joshua marched in. "I don't know what you're up to," he said, "and I don't care. You're making the bank look bad and we can't have it."

I doubted any customers were asking questions, and if they were, it would be easy enough to say the detectives were here investigating credit card fraud or a stolen identity or someone trying to break into the ATM.

"You need to go home," Joshua said. "And think about whether this job is a good fit for you."

Before I left, I changed the beneficiary on my life insurance.

I'd bought a gun just before the pandemic, without saying anything to Tony. I'd also bought nine bullets, though I only planned to use one. At some point, when the world became too much to bear, I'd go out in the back yard and pull the trigger.

I knew the time to buy the pistol was *before* things got desperate.

Three years and I'd never oiled it once. I hoped the damn thing still worked.

Moralists didn't want to make Death with Dignity meds available to those with depression, but that decision had always felt oppressive to me, not the work of an ally.

An ally would get us universal mental healthcare *first* and then worry about the rest. Otherwise, we were trapped, like a comatose quadriplegic who was fully aware of his surroundings.

I managed not to stop by Elijah's camper on the way home, though I couldn't resist picking up a couple of apples and knocking on the door of a truck cab half a block down the hill from him. The black man who answered looked at the apples suspiciously but took them, along with a bottle of water.

Plastic.

I arrived at the house long before Tony was due back from work. I opened the closet to look at his clothes, stuck my hand in his underwear drawer to feel the cotton, and looked at his artwork on the wall. Early in our relationship, he'd commissioned a charcoal of me in the sling, my asshole facing the artist, my feet in leather stirrups. Tony had hated our trip to Italy two years later but had framed a photo of me standing next to the citofono of our Bed and Breakfast.

I lurked online sometimes and saw the routine MAGA posts from family members. What Tony and I needed, though, was a MORGAN campaign—Make Our Relationship Great Again…Now!

Thank God we'd never been legally married. Though I suppose the fact that same-sex marriage had been legal for a decade and we'd never taken advantage of it said something about the state of our relationship even then.

I remembered the relief I'd felt at my Court of Love when the stake president declared me excommunicated and ordered me to take off my underwear. He'd wanted me to step into an adjacent room to remove the sacred undergarments, but I'd started stripping right on the spot. The entire High Council had fled the room.

I called the realtor and asked him to come to the house on Thursday, my next day off. Assuming I wouldn't be fired the moment I arrived at the bank tomorrow morning.

***

"My friends can't believe I hang with you guys so much," Valentina said. She put an N at the end of "diva."

"Not everyone has interesting parents," Roger pointed out. He made the word "gate" with the G on a double letter score.

"Fun parents," Krichelle added. She added a D to Roger's word.

"Parents that are too cringe to hang out with in public," I said, placing an N and an E in front of Krichelle's latest version of Roger's word.

"Pot!" Valentina laughed. "Kettle! Black!" It was always dangerous to tease, but Roger and Krichelle laughed, too.

We were about halfway through our game of Scrabble, and I hadn't said anything yet about the latest developments. Sometimes, it was nice to pretend to be normal. But other times, you needed a little comfort, a little validation. So I finally caught them up on the news.

Roger leaned back from the table, his face expressionless. Krichelle folded her arms and frowned.

Valentina leaned forward eagerly.

Then Roger spoke. "Uh, look, Morgan," he began. "I know it's terrible that homeless man was killed."

"Nick," I said.

"But you need to let it go. It's not worth putting yourself in danger. And it's certainly not worth putting other people in danger."

"We don't know that the receptionist's death is connected to Nick's," I said.

Roger started to say something but stopped. He looked at Krichelle, and she took over. "This is just an intellectual exercise for you, Morgan." She shrugged. "Maybe you're getting a sense of moral justice out of it. You lead a dull life like most of us, and this makes you feel important."

"Jesus, Mom."

"But neither of those is worth risking our daughter's safety."

"Excuse me?"

"You need to stay away for a while, Morgan." Krichelle stood up, with Roger following immediately. Valentina sat with her mouth open.

Part of me understood they were right, but I couldn't stop myself. I seemed to be having an out-of-body experience, watching from a tall height as a second me spiraled out of control in a torn hang glider plummeting to the ground.

I started picking up tiles and slipping them into their velvet bag. "Roger, do you tell black people, 'Hey, I know white people treat you badly, but that's just life. Deal with it?'"

I hadn't realized that the charcoal of my asshole had captured the real me so effectively.

"What?"

"Krichelle, do you tell a woman who's been raped that the criminal justice system will make her regret coming forward and she just has to suck it up?"

"Jesus, Morgan."

"It's okay if life stinks for others, as long as *we* don't have to do anything about it."

"You need to leave *right now*."

***

When I walked through our front door, Tony was sitting on the sofa watching television. "I knew you wouldn't be home when I got back from work," he said. "I thought about calling first, but I needed to see if you'd step up." He still hadn't looked away from the television. "You failed the test."

I walked to the kitchen and poured myself some kombucha.

"Last week, I started wearing a new cologne, and you didn't notice," he went on. "The week before that, I moved the vase from the living room to the dining nook, and you didn't notice."

The words stung, mostly because they were true. It took two to ruin a relationship. "Our marriage would have been far stronger," I said, "if you hadn't invested so much energy in testing my worthiness to be with you."

I wondered if he noticed the verb tense.

Tony stood up, still without looking at me, grabbed his keys, and walked out the door. For all I knew, he'd find an apartment before the realtor ever showed up.

Maybe things were finally starting to go my way.

I brushed my teeth, put on my sweats, and sat on the front porch in the dark. A bus ran up Renton a block over. A car door slammed somewhere toward the cross street. The branches of the service berry tree in the front yard rustled softly in the breeze.

If I was renting and didn't have equity in the house when Joshua fired me, I could be homeless myself in a matter of weeks.

That was the real reason people hated seeing the unhoused. It was easier to hate those on the margins than acknowledge the failed system that created those margins, easier to fear the miserable than to build a system that no longer forced so many people into misery.

It was the same reason Mormons abandoned their gay and trans family members. It was easier to stop loving than accept they'd been deceived by their leaders.

Affinity fraud.

A shot rang out in the distance, and somewhere a dog started barking.

Chapter Eighteen: Lining up the Sights

I experienced a doomscrolling relapse the following morning, reading about the discovery of a mass grave in Ukraine with over 440 bodies. A former Trump cabinet member announced on a right-wing news show that state governors had the right to declare war against domestic enemies, which included pretty much everyone who wasn't a Trump supporter.

More than one evangelical preacher was claiming that Trump was the "Son of Man." They acknowledged that Jesus was still the Son of God but insisted Trump was the Messiah who would usher in Armageddon and the Second Coming.

I remembered my Seminary instructor telling us that if we had our Two-Year Supply of food and other essentials, we didn't need to fear the future. The Second Coming couldn't happen until there was worldwide destruction, so we had to hope and pray that destruction came soon.

Self-fulfilling prophecy was still prophecy, I supposed.

I'd read the book *Paradise* by Lizzie Johnson, about the wildfire that destroyed the town of 26,000 people in a matter of hours. She talked about three phases of responding to disaster. The longest phase was denial, with some people referencing their past experiences to predict the current one. "The last four hurricanes veered away at the last minute, so I'm not going to evacuate." By the time people realized *this* disaster was different, it was often too late.

I received dozens of political emails every day. One this morning contained a cartoon showing two Jews in line heading to the gas chambers. There was a smoking chimney in the background. One man comments, "Hitler sure is horrible. Someone should do something."

The other man says, "Oh, let's not talk about politics. It's so divisive."

Godwin's Law. But even a broken clock marked the correct time twice a day.

Krichelle and Roger were right. Who was I to be Nick's savior or Elijah's savior or anyone else's? With my increasingly lackluster life, I was only trying to reframe my self-image, see myself as a decent guy when I really contributed almost nothing toward making the world a better place.

It wasn't as if I was running for office, trying to get on the City Council to address housing. I couldn't even muster the strength to attend Seattle Public Transit

Advisory Board meetings. I kept putting them on my calendar each month and then skipping them.

Though I supposed running for a local office wouldn't hurt. I didn't need to win to bring up important issues. Bernie showed us that.

I was going to be late for work, and after yesterday, I couldn't afford to upset Joshua any further. I got dressed and ran out the door.

Damn. My big toe had worn a hole in the top of my right shoe. So unprofessional.

***

Luck was with me this morning. I grabbed the seat on the right side of the bus just before the rear door, the row with the most leg room of any on the bus. Even I wasn't fat enough to need all that space, but it was relaxing not to feel cramped, and to know I was only inches from the exit when the time came.

From the rear of the bus, a black man kept repeating, "My niece is eight! My niece is eight! My niece is eight!"

Somewhere on the spectrum?

No one seemed to hear the man. Or see him. Public transit riders were the wisest of the Japanese "See no evil, hear no evil, speak no evil" monkeys.

So I was surprised when an elderly Filipina across the aisle from me opened her purse, took out a wrapped candy, and walked to the back of the bus. A few of us did turn to watch her hand it to the man with an eight-year-old niece before she walked back up to her original seat.

Krichelle's words had disappointed me. I never expected a lot of strength from men. Too many times, a partner had told me he loved me and then broken up with me days later. Even if Krichelle was right, she'd inflicted pain.

Her words hurt more *because* she was right.

A young Latino in work clothes boarded and sat next to me, manspreading so forcefully he nudged my left leg against my right.

"I appreciate you spreading your legs for easy access," I said loudly, "but don't you think it would be more appropriate to do in private?"

I'd become another crazy old man on the bus.

***

Joshua walked up to me as soon as I entered the door at the bank. "You better be on your best behavior today."

"You mean...really good at catching murderers?"

No sense cowering.

Mirelle wasn't wearing earrings this morning, but I wasn't up to asking why. I helped a customer cancel a debit card and order a new one, something she could have done over the phone. But she was elderly and lonely, and we chatted about her parakeets while I conducted her request.

I ate a vanilla Greek yogurt for lunch. Two grams of fat, three grams of carbs, and twelve grams of protein.

Not fifteen minutes after I returned to my window, Detectives Stalder and Klimczyk walked into the building. "We're going to need you to come with us," Klimczyk said.

"What?"

"We're bringing you in for questioning," Stalder explained. "For the murder of Elijah Thomas."

I braced myself on the counter in front of me. Elijah was dead, too?

"I…I talked to him briefly on Sunday," I said. "He wasn't in the mood to talk."

"A witness says Mr. Thomas told him he was tired of you coming around and told you to back off." Stalder's eyes were unflinching.

I nodded. "That's true."

"Mr. Beylerian, perhaps it's best we continue this conversation down at the station." Klimczyk motioned for me to move toward the end of the teller line. I realized that Mirelle, Jevin, Joshua, Shanifer, and three customers were all staring at me as if I'd turned green.

I logged off the computer and waved goodbye to Mirelle. Joshua would have to count my drawer, and I'd have to hope he didn't deliberately sabotage me. At this point, of course, he hardly needed any more justification to fire me.

The detectives didn't handcuff me, and no one used the word "arrested," but I still felt I was heading to the gallows as I climbed into the back seat of their car. I remembered teaching Gheorghe Petrescu in Rome after he'd escaped Romania. And how he'd disappeared from his hostel one hour before our sixth scheduled visit, his few belongings still in his room.

Neither Stalder nor Klimczyk spoke during the ride to Othello. Walking through the station, I was surprised to notice how small it seemed, like a TV set and not like one at the same time.

I could really use some otherworldly advice from Cagliostro.

Soon we were in an interrogation room, quite small. The requisite two-way mirror hung on one wall. But really, it was just a one-way mirror, wasn't it? From the other side it was just a window. Why did everyone call it a two-way mirror?

"Did you kill Elijah Thomas?" Detective Stalder asked.

Right to the point. Good. "No." Nothing to elaborate on.

"Your fingerprints are all over his camper."

"I thought we already established that I visited him multiple times."

"Why was Mr. Thomas afraid of you?" Stalder asked.

I couldn't keep from chuckling at the amateurish attempt. "He didn't want me to visit more than once a week. That's all I usually visited Nick, but after Nick was killed, I couldn't keep from trying to talk to his neighbors to learn something that might be useful."

"Uh huh."

"Was Elijah's throat slit, too?"

"You tell me."

I shrugged. Elijah had said he had some shady history, so his murder might be completely unrelated to Nick's. But even if that were true, no one would buy such a thing now, with three possibly related murders in a row.

"Someone saw you pause yesterday by Elijah's camper but not stop. Was that when you decided to come back later and kill him?"

"Are you sure the guy who accused me didn't do it?" I asked. I didn't know any of the other names along that stretch of road, and I had no idea if the guy I'd given the apples to was the one who said anything or not.

How in the world did real detectives piece all this stuff together?

"Are we going to find another homeless man you don't like dead?" Stalder asked.

"What makes you think there are homeless men I don't like?" I asked. "They all have dicks, don't they?"

He meant to intimidate me, I supposed, but by asking that question, he was already telling me he wasn't keeping me here. I remembered the tactics my mission president had used in our quarterly interviews. "The Spirit has told me there's something you need to repent of." Just taking a wild stab that twenty-year-old men would have done or thought something inappropriate at least once in the past four months. I always answered by saying something like, "There was a man I thought I should approach on the sidewalk to get a referral, and I didn't do it because I wanted to get home for lunch."

There was rarely anything "real" to confess. It wasn't as if I so much as masturbated during those two years.

Well, not much.

The president would admonish me, I'd promise to do better, and then I'd be dismissed so the president could torture another young soul.

"I don't understand what's going on," I said. "If Elijah was killed because of Nick, did he know too much? He told me he didn't like talking to the police, but I think he would have told me if he knew something."

"Because you were so close?"

He had a point.

"Do you think he was killed to implicate me in Nick's murder?" I asked. It sounded so convoluted. If I was a threat to the murderer, why not just kill me?

Because that would prove Nick's murderer was still at large.

"Have you checked where Erik Marklund was at the time of the murder?" And now I sounded just like every guilty character trying to misdirect one of Anna-Maria Giovanoli's investigations. "When *was* he murdered?" If it was in the middle of the night, I'd have no alibi, either. Not even an unreliable one from a partner.

I explained my actions of the past twenty-four hours, giving them Tony's cell number and that of Krichelle and Roger as well. "But please don't call the Dugas," I said. "They're already freaked by Elodie's murder and are afraid I'm getting people around me killed."

"You are," Klimczyk said.

"Or you're killing them yourself."

The questioning continued in much the same manner for another hour, but there was nothing new for me to add. Stalder was sure he could trip me up and kept trying to find inconsistencies in my account, but I'd done so little there wasn't much for me to keep track of.

"If there's anything at all you need to tell us," Stalder said, "now is the time."

My first time through the temple, an officiator had addressed the room of forty adults about to start the endowment ceremony. "If you have any unresolved sin, you can leave the room now without any shame and talk to a priesthood authority. If you don't resolve the sin, we'll know when it's time for you to pass through the veil, and we won't be able to let you into the Celestial Room."

I'd had years of experience keeping my face expressionless under pressure.

But I still wasn't prepared for what came next.

Chapter Nineteen: Cocking the Hammer

"Mr. Beylerian, eighteen homeless men have been murdered in Seattle so far this year."

I rubbed my arms. They kept this room so cold.

"We're wondering if some of them weren't targeted by a serial killer."

And suddenly, I realized the detectives didn't suspect me at all. They simply needed "a win" to show their superiors and the rest of the city they were doing their job. This was a Lose-Win-Win for them.

I said nothing.

"Mr. Beylerian," Stalder continued, "no jury in the world will think the testimony of a freak who has sex with homeless men is trustworthy."

"I'm also not terribly cheerful or reverent."

"They don't trust former prostitutes, either," he added.

"I expect you're right," I replied. "Odd, though, how juries still believe the testimony of police officers, even when we've all seen hours and hours of video of uniformed men killing people and then lying about it."

It was impossible for police brutality not to be one of the issues important to me, but now was hardly the time to bring it up. If they beat me to death, though, or staged my suicide in a jail cell, all this misery might finally be over.

For me, anyway.

"You little—"

"I'm quite big, in case you hadn't noticed."

I heard the Osmonds singing "One Bad Apple." Theirs was the first concert I ever attended, when I was just ten.

I remembered Chris Rock's comment about bad apples.

Detective Klimczyk pulled his partner aside and motioned toward the door. "We're going to leave you here to reconsider your attitude," Klimczyk said, "and we'll continue our questioning later." The two men left.

"Et tu?" I asked the empty room. I looked at the mirror on the wall and flossed between my teeth with a thumbnail.

I remembered attending my 10th high school reunion and feeling surprised everyone's personality seemed exactly the same. There'd been no apparent growth whatsoever. I'd noticed the same thing with my grandparents and great-aunts and -uncles approaching death. I'd expected them to make one last effort to be decent to those they were leaving behind. But only the people who were already kind acted kindly. The jerks remained jerks to the bitter end.

I guess I was one of the jerks.

I'd so wanted to be a good guy, even after I realized there was no reward for it.

Well, I did get a few endorphins from thinking I'd made someone's day slightly better. My favorite Dickens quote was, "No one is useless in this world who lightens the burden of it for anyone else." As good as anything from the Sermon on the Mount. Another of the quotes I periodically posted over my home computer.

But didn't Dickens die unhappy?

Maybe I'd have time to write more op-eds from prison, perhaps learn how to draw. I'd always wanted to create political cartoons. I'd draw two emaciated men in a devastated city, bodies all around them. One man says to the other, "I'd have done more about climate change if the activists had used a nicer tone."

You know, something funny.

I heard a tap on the mirror and looked over, but I couldn't see anyone on the other side. The detectives had let me call Tony when they brought me in, but it had gone to voice mail, so I didn't know if he'd even listened to it yet.

I'd always thought I'd be married for "time and all eternity." Even in gay years, seventeen wasn't eternity.

"You'll rue the day you chose homosexuality over the gospel," was the first thing my bishop had said when I came out to him. The second was, "Do you have sex with dogs?"

I'd been flabbergasted. Surely, he wasn't asking about sexual positions, was he? "You mean doggy style anal sex?" I'd asked.

Bishop Hauer had shuddered. "Of course not. I'm asking if you have sex with dogs."

"Only Neapolitan mastiffs," I'd said with a straight face. The bishop seemed to believe me.

"Morgan, you're disfellowshipped immediately. You're not allowed to participate in class or offer prayers or take the sacrament while you wait for your trial."

I hadn't been attending church much by that point anyway, but it had been surprisingly difficult to break away, despite its toxicity. The mindset was all encompassing. I wasn't sure I could have broken away at all if I hadn't *had* to.

"You're not allowed to pay tithing, either. No blessings for you."

"I guess I'll have to spend the money on dildos," I'd responded with a sigh. "And hand them out to poor gay guys so it'll still count as charity in God's eyes."

Was that how I'd started down this path? Was my life a joke?

After an hour in the empty interrogation room, I started feeling an urgency in my bladder but refused to knock on the door or wave at the window. If worse came to worst, I was not above pissing in a trash can or in the corner.

I'd pissed in more compromising locations.

During my exit interview in Rome, President Ryssman had told me, "You were always easy, Anziano Beylerian. I never had to worry about you."

He was in his nineties now, still alive and living in Salt Lake. I rarely posted to my mission Facebook group. When I did, it was news of the mudslide in Ischia or about a new discovery in Pompeii or photos of the Po drying up. When one of my former district leaders asked how I knew so much about what was currently happening in Italy, I replied that I watched RAI and France 24 and DW.

It had never occurred to him he could watch non-American news.

Okay. I couldn't hold it any longer. I stood up and walked over to the trash can.

The door opened. When I turned to look for the detectives, I did a double take worthy of Marie Dressler. "Officer Tockner."

He smiled grimly and walked over to me. "Your friend is out front to take you home."

"Tony?"

Tockner frowned. "Someone named Krichelle."

"Oh."

"I don't know what's going on," Tockner said, "but I know you are not going to do well in lock-up."

I'm tough, I wanted to say. I'm a big boy. I'm a survivor.

And now all I could think of was Beyoncé.

"Let's get you out of here."

"I need to piss."

Tockner smiled. He'd confided some of his fantasies but we'd never done anything other than straight oral.

I suddenly realized he was outing himself by coming into the room.

"Thank you," I said.

"This isn't over." He led me to the door. "You're not under arrest…yet, but you need to watch yourself."

I nodded.

"I'll call once you've been fully cleared."

After a quick trip to the restroom, where we pissed side by side, Tockner led me out front to meet Krichelle. It was 5:30, though it felt much later. I wondered what Roger thought about his wife's decision to come to the station, if she'd consulted with him or made the decision on her own.

There was some sudden commotion and several officers ran out of the building. I heard sirens in the distance. Krichelle and I watched as three cars sped off.

Once, I'd seen twelve police cars—twelve!—flying past the #7 on Rainier, lights flashing and sirens blaring. An active shooter, I'd wondered? A terrorist attack?

Turned out it was a car chase for someone who'd fled a traffic stop. The driver had an outstanding warrant for unpaid fines.

The justice system was a blunt tool. Just like chemotherapy aimed to get rid of diseased tissue but also damaged healthy cells, it was unrealistic to expect accuracy and perfection. But just as we vowed to refine cancer treatment to target the specific cells we wanted to kill, it was wrong to shrug away friendly fire casualties on our own streets, in our own homes.

Walking out of the police station didn't make me feel free.

My mom's type of leukemia was almost completely treatable today.

"Are you okay, Morgan?"

I closed my eyes. "Sure."

"Tony told me a little when I went over to apologize." She shook her head. "We all said some things we regret, I'm sure."

"Yes."

Sometimes, medical treatments were abandoned altogether in favor of a completely new approach.

"I still think we were right," Krichelle went on. She motioned to the station around us. "This is not good."

"No."

"But we still couldn't leave you here. Tony…"

"Don't worry about Tony."

She nodded.

"And given the circumstances, I'd better tell you while I have a chance that you and Roger are the beneficiaries on my life insurance."

Krichelle blinked.

"I didn't want you catching the bus home," she said. "I've got the car out front. Let's go."

***

Krichelle drove me home. It took six minutes. I caught her up on the details Tony didn't know and was relieved when she didn't threaten to cut me off again. She and Roger at least had a home alarm system. Tony refused to pay for one and I couldn't afford an alarm on my own.

"I may call to vent over the next few days," I said as I stepped out of the car, "but I don't expect to leave the house at all except to go to work until the police find the killer."

"No more detective work?"

I shrugged. I hadn't really done much to begin with.

"Maybe we can Zoom a Scrabble game."

I smiled, only then realizing I wasn't wearing my mask. Krichelle hadn't been wearing one, either. "You guys play without me," I said. "Just be sure to use the word 'bypass' at some point." I needed to spend the upcoming evenings watching weight loss and nutrition videos. Pedaling on my stationary bike as I did so.

I walked up to the house, pausing at the door. I did not have the energy for another argument.

There was no God to bargain with, nothing I could agree to do or give up to bring the murderer to justice.

If I tried really, really hard, if Tony and I went to couples counseling, if I could finally lose some weight, perhaps our relationship was still salvageable. But if the past few days had taught me anything, it was not to waste the little time I had left on the planet. That meant making some big decisions. And that was scary because I would be stuck with those decisions probably for the rest of my life.

I supposed the only consolation for making a mistake was that almost every decision, bad *or* good, had unexpected negative consequences. Accepting a promotion, moving to a new neighborhood, even winning the lottery.

If I didn't make *this* mistake, I was sure to make *that* one. It was inevitable. As long as I chose something that at least had a few relevant good points, the rest was just collateral life damage.

I unlocked the door and walked into the living room. Tony sat on the sofa, eating a sandwich while watching TV. "Get fucked by any homeless guys in jail?" he asked.

I shook my head. "Just a gang bang by five police officers."

He looked at me. "You think you're so funny."

"The realtor will be here on Thursday."

Tony's eyes narrowed. "That another joke?"

"Nope."

"Well, I'm going to get *my* money out of this place first," he said, jabbing his index finger in my direction.

"Why don't you take the fridge?" I suggested. "And I'll take the sling."

"What for? Nobody wants to fuck *your* fat ass."

Probably not. But it might be a comfortable place to rest if I decided to overdose on insulin. That wasn't the most pleasant way to go, but even employed beggars couldn't be choosers.

"You think you're so good," Tony went on, "but good people don't ruin—"

My cell phone rang, and I pulled it out of my pocket. I didn't get calls often. The Caller ID said "Unknown." It might be Tockner. I swiped the green Answer button.

"Hello?"

"Mr. Beylerian?" a male voice asked.

"Yes?"

"It's Steven J. Akerstrom. Do you have a moment to chat?"

I covered the phone with my hand. "I have to take this," I said. "But let's finish our conversation first."

"Okay." Tony stood up defiantly.

"Get out." I thrust my thumb over my shoulder toward the door. Then I put the phone back up to my face. "Mr. Akerstrom?"

"Mr. Beylerian." The voice sounded serious. "I have some important news about Nicholas Degraff."

Chapter Twenty: Pulling the Trigger

"I apologize for the delay in responding to your email," Akerstrom began, "but this *is* pro bono work, after all."

"I appreciate you responding at all," I said. And frankly, I was glad he hadn't called earlier. Before I met Tony, I'd enjoyed jigsaw puzzles, but it was difficult to find any with 500 pieces that weren't aimed at kids. Most of the interesting photos had 750 or 1000 or 2000 pieces, and even if I chose something without a huge expanse of sky or millions of tiny flowers, it just wasn't fun working with so many pieces.

"I was a bit surprised to find your email in my inbox," Akerstrom went on. "Nick told me he hadn't informed you about the money."

"Excuse me?"

"The trust isn't set up to distribute funds until January, but I suppose there's no reason not to tell you what you'll be receiving."

I almost asked another question but stopped myself before revealing any more of my ignorance that might shut him down.

"There are only five beneficiaries," Akerstrom said. "You and his wife will receive the same amount, $25,000 each. Nick's two kids will each receive the bulk of the funds, just over $120,000 each. And the last recipient is a leukemia foundation that will receive $10,000."

I felt dizzy and sat down. "Mr. Akerstrom," I managed, "if Nick had $300,000 why are you working pro bono?"

Akerstrom sighed. "We knew each other from church," he explained. "He used to visit me once a month, no matter what, and he helped me through a rough patch when I questioned my faith after my wife left me." He chuckled. "Sorry, TMI."

I closed my eyes. It made perfect sense that Nick had been a devoted Home Teacher, one of the most hated callings in the Mormon religion. I remembered the online hubbub when it was abolished a few years earlier. Rejoicing throughout the land.

"If I can ask one more question," I said, "why did Nick live in a camper if he had all that money?"

"I can't answer that one, I'm afraid. He only told me about the cryptocurrency two weeks ago. He gave me instructions on how to convert it and then divvy it up."

We chatted for just a few more minutes, the attorney promising to contact me again the first week of January. After the call, I gazed absentmindedly out my window at the Ethiopian church across the street. Women in white shawls were heading to the rear entrance.

Had Nick embezzled the money, I wondered? Was that the reason he'd been fired? If the funds were acquired illegally, though, the company would have simply had him arrested. Mr. Gustafson had said something about Nick signing a contract that lost the company money, but that wouldn't have gained Nick any of those funds. And if someone had been forging his name, Nick would have been more likely to lose his job *and* his money rather than gain anything.

But that was all for the detectives to sort out. I realized I'd never told them about the attorney, realized that telling them now would only strengthen any motive I had for killing Nick in the first place. But there was no getting around it. I dialed Klimczyk's number, and when he answered, I filled him in on the latest information.

"Will you be coming to pick me up again?" I asked.

Klimczyk was silent a moment. "Not tonight, Mr. Beylerian. Try to have a good night's sleep."

***

I remembered the time Elder Grant had run off with Napoli Two's district money. Each month, the four or six elders sharing an apartment would pool our funds, and then the district leader would pay the rent and utilities. Each Preparation Day, he'd hand out that week's food allowance to the missionary assigned to cook for the week.

The first of the month, Elder Grant had stolen the district money and run off in the middle of the night. We'd all assumed he'd headed for the airport—the church wouldn't pay our ticket home if we left before our two years were up—but Elder Grant had instead hired four prostitutes who hung out near the Ospedale Cardarelli and spent all night with them in a hotel in the Chiaia.

He didn't need to pay his way home, after all.

I really wanted a low-carb pot brownie.

Or some mushrooms.

Even a psychotherapist.

If taxes could pay for public defenders, why couldn't they cover public therapists so that we needed fewer public defenders?

I moved out to the front porch and watched a squirrel hunt for a nut it had buried somewhere near the service berry tree. He was not having any success. A cloud drifted slowly past the moon. The neighbor's cat crept across my front path, paused to inspect me, and kept walking. I looked toward the street as a sage green sedan pulled over in front of the house.

Officer Tockner stepped out of the car wearing civilian clothes. I nodded and he walked up to the porch. "Can I come inside?"

I almost made a joke but it was clear neither of us was in the mood for puns. I stood and motioned him to follow. "Would you like something to drink?" I asked. "I have seltzer water or protein shakes."

He shook his head, so I led him to the sofa. He sat right next to me, his knee pressing against mine. "Why are you here?" I finally asked.

Tockner smiled. "I got a good bit of grief today after going into the interrogation room," he said, "but when I told the other officers very calmly that you and I were fuck buddies, they backed off." He puffed his cheeks and blew out some air, making a noise that didn't sound particularly triumphant. "No telling what things'll be like tomorrow, but…"

I remembered the time Karow was secretly filmed getting fucked and was teased mercilessly by the other officers in Berlin. He'd simply told them, "I bet I had better sex than you did last night," and left it at that.

"I heard enough to know the basics of your situation," Tockner went on. "I know no one really knows another person, and we barely talked the times we met." He put his hand on my shoulder. "But I'll be here for you, whatever comes out."

"Why?" I asked. "I'm no one." Old and fat and poor, or at least not middle class. Even the best sex, and I sure never gave anyone that, couldn't merit the risks he'd taken today.

"You *did* something," he said.

I frowned.

"Most people walk on by. You stopped."

"I'm not sure—"

"Look," Tockner said, "most people will never save anyone from a burning car or stop an armed robbery. But anyone can mow the lawn for their neighbor or pick up packages from their porch while they're away." He smiled. "But most don't even talk to them."

Well, I did pick up my neighbor's packages for them, but I didn't mow their lawn.

"Every person is the center of their own universe, so when you do even a small thing for that center, the universe feels it."

I put my hand on my forehead to tamp down a growing headache. I never thought of police officers as especially philosophical, despite Captain Marleau's musings.

The actress who portrayed her had lived on the streets for a few years before finding a job in theater.

"You brought food to a homeless man, Morgan, and you tried to find whoever killed him. You took a lot of chances, and maybe you'll go down for it, but I can tell you this, I don't see that kind of thing often, so when I do, I notice."

I didn't know what to say to any of that. He was right and he was wrong and none of it mattered anyway. "I just wish…" I said. "I wish…"

Tockner leaned back on the sofa and pulled my head to his shoulder, wrapping an arm around me. Neither of us said any more, sitting in silence for another fifteen minutes. He finally pulled away and stood up.

"I really do need to go," he said, "and I may not be able to talk to you for a few days, depending on how things shake out, but I needed you to know you're not going to slip through the cracks and be forgotten."

I expected he meant that to sound more comforting than it did. "Thanks."

"Peter," he said.

"Peter."

"You already know why I only go by P, but I figured it was time to tell you my full name."

I stood as well and led him to the door. He paused to kiss me on the cheek and then headed out to his car.

I did *not* want to date again. Ever. But it sure would be nice to have the kind of friend Peter might just turn out to be.

***

I couldn't muster more than a few spoonfuls of active culture cottage cheese for dinner, washing that down with a bit of kombucha. The good news, though, was that I was down to 215 pounds. Only…two more pounds to go.

I'd watched all the medical videos I could stomach, read a chapter from the next installment of Maz Maddox's dinosaur shapeshifter series, and even watched an episode of *Crime Scene Cleaner*, the one where Schotty gets trapped in a magician's disappearing cabinet with the dead man's lover. I still didn't feel sleepy. Would calling in sick tomorrow hurt or help my chances of staying with the bank?

The money Nick had left me wasn't enough to retire on, yet with the sale of the house, I could probably rent an apartment in Italy for a few years, make it to sixty-five, anyway. Assuming I wasn't in prison. Assuming I'd even get to keep the money. And if I ran out of funds and needed to kill myself then, so be it. I'd at least have had a little happiness at the end of my life.

Not that Italy didn't have its own problems, as clearly evidenced in *Lampedusa*, but for God's sake, I lived in Seattle, the home of Amazon and Microsoft and Starbucks and Boeing and Costco, some of the most successful corporations in the country, even in the entire world, and we couldn't manage to raise enough taxes to keep huge swaths of the city indistinguishable from Third World countries.

I turned out the light but remained on the sofa. I didn't want to sleep in the bed I used to share with Tony, didn't really even want to dream. Every little while, a bus rumbled up or down Renton. Something skittered across our roof. An acorn fell on the tiny air conditioner hanging out the living room window.

My eyes burned just a bit when I closed them. It was time to apply a heated rice compress again to the stye but I didn't want to move off the sofa. I sighed, fantasizing about sliding my name into the citofono of my new apartment, maybe in Cremona, and eventually, I drifted off to sleep.

Sometime later, I woke up, debating whether or not I could wait until morning to head to the bathroom. When my glucose was fully under control, I could make it through the night. But this wasn't one of those nights, despite my light dinner.

I started to push off the sofa with my arms out of habit but stopped myself, using only my legs instead. I had to stand a moment to make sure I could balance, and to make sure I didn't do anything to spark another case of plantar fasciitis. There was always something. Just as I was about to take a step, I heard a noise.

The sound was coming from inside the house.

I'd identified with Carol Kane when I'd first seen the movie. Now I was Charles Durning.

The noise didn't repeat, so I took a step. And then I heard it again. Something was in the basement. I'd pestered Tony to help me hire someone to block all the tiny entryways into the house. I hated when we had squirrels or birds in the attic, and I sure didn't want rats coming in. But Tony hadn't wanted to pay anything, I couldn't afford it by myself, and I certainly wasn't up to the manual labor.

Two more sounds in a row.

Those were *footsteps*.

Tony coming home in the middle of the night? Or…

My pistol was at the bottom of my office closet under a folded blanket. The law required gunowners to keep guns unloaded and secured. Mine was in a lockbox, the key on my keyring. I wasn't sure I remembered where the bullets were. In the lockbox as well?

More steps. Someone was coming up the basement stairs. I remembered when Adeline was kidnapped, when Isabel was strangled. I was finally going to meet Nick's killer. I'd never have to worry about a bone marrow biopsy or going into convulsions from too much insulin.

Maybe I'd even see my mom again.

Then I remembered the time two men had attacked Elder Welty and me in the Rione Sanità. I'd just bought a cameo of the Angel Moroni—the artists at De Paola knew how to keep the Mormon missionaries coming back—and those bastards weren't going to take my mom's birthday present. I'd grabbed a wooden chair an old woman had just vacated when the attack began and swung it with all my might.

I picked up the coffee table in front of me and charged through the kitchen toward the top of the basement stairs as if I was trying to break down a castle gate with a battering ram. I struck something so hard I lost my breath and collapsed against the counter, knocking the coffee pot to the floor, where it shattered with a sharp, piercing crash.

I felt my chest to see if I'd broken a rib, if a splintered fragment of wood had stabbed me. I still couldn't catch my breath. Did I have a collapsed lung? Was I going to have a heart attack like a football player after a tackle? My chest was on fire.

Maybe I'd killed myself after all.

I barely heard the sound of someone tumbling down the basement stairs.

But some remote part of my brain did hear him shout. It wasn't Tony.

My left hand still pressed against my sternum, I staggered to the light switch and flipped it on. At the bottom of the steps, propped awkwardly against the washing machine, was Harold Gustafson. He groaned loudly, raised one arm in my direction, and fired.

Chapter Twenty-One: Gluttony in Moderation

Detectives Stalder and Klimczyk came to the hospital Wednesday morning to ask more questions, but they didn't answer many of mine. It was unclear if the original scandal attributed to Nick had in fact been committed by Nick or a forger, but that incident didn't seem directly related to any of the killings. There'd been a ransomware attack a few weeks back, and that seemed unrelated, too, except that it appeared to have pushed Harold into a string of revenge killings, even if none of his targets had anything to do with the attack.

"Over a year ago, Mr. Degraff encouraged Mr. Gustafson to invest in the company, and with all the trouble lately, he lost most of his savings. The company is on the verge of bankruptcy."

"So he lashed out at two homeless men, a receptionist, and me?" I asked. Like an angry young man randomly killing nineteen children and two adults in Uvalde. Senseless.

Why not kill Mr. Marklund, I wondered. The guy was such an asshole, anyway. Why not try to kill whoever opened the company up to the ransomware?

"Toxicology will tell us if Mr. Gustafson was impaired," Klimczyk said, "or if he had a brain tumor or some other health issue."

Harold had died from bleeding in his brain on the way to the hospital. Even completely dazed, he'd managed to shoot me in the abdomen. Tony had gotten his wish. And I suppose I did, too. Half my stomach was removed. Fortunately, the fact that I'd eaten so lightly helped reduce my risk of infection.

It was hard to tell, but it felt like the surgeon might have removed some of the fat as well. In any event, I chose to believe he did and hoped for a placebo effect, determined to make the most of the situation. I'd get down to 200 pounds and then reevaluate.

"Do we know it was him?" I pressed. "He slit Nick's throat, and you just told me Elijah and Elodie were stabbed to death. Why would Harold come after me with a gun?"

"Why would he come after you at all if he wasn't responsible for the other murders?" Stalder asked with a slight roll of his eyes.

The bad cop routine apparently wasn't an act.

I asked more questions, but the detectives either didn't know the answers or didn't feel it worth their time to share any with me. What had Elodie meant by her "net zero" musing? Had she obtained an abortion? Did she merely feel guilty for not having helped the homeless man who died near the building entrance five days before anyone noticed?

Perhaps it wasn't a coincidence that Harold appeared at my teller window. Maybe he was worried after I showed up at Nick's workplace and started asking questions. For all I knew, there really were security cameras and he was trying to implicate me if any suspicions came his way. Or he might simply have been trying to find out if I knew anything.

Maybe it was Elodie seeing me there on friendly terms with Harold that made her a liability.

Maybe Nick and Harold had planned the malware attack together and Nick had double-crossed him.

Or maybe Harold merely suspected Nick was responsible for the ransomware attack but didn't have enough proof to go to the police.

Maybe he'd gone to Nick's camper to confront him and things spiraled out of control.

This was getting to be another 750-piece puzzle even after we knew who the killer was.

Inspector LaBrea had always been able to wrap things up neatly after ninety minutes. Maybe in real life, things were never quite as tidy.

"We'll type up your statement and have you sign it later," Klimczyk said. "And Mr. Beylerian?"

"Yes?"

"I hope you've gotten amateur sleuthing out of your system."

"Am I still an amateur, though?" I asked. "I did help you catch the murderer."

"You got shot and *we* caught the murderer," Stalder corrected.

"I'm still adding this to the Miscellaneous Skills section of my resumé."

Klimczyk turned to hide a smile, while Stalder grunted and motioned for his partner to follow him into the hallway. Klimczyk paused at the door a moment and then returned to my bedside.

"Be nice to P," he said. "He's a good guy."

I frowned. "Uh, were you two…?"

Klimczyk shrugged. "Too complicated to see someone at work," he said.

"Maybe we'll invite you over for a movie sometime," I said. "Do you like Polish detective shows?"

I cringed. Why in the world had I used the pronoun "we"? Tony hadn't even responded to my messages yet.

While it wouldn't be hard to stop thinking of him as my partner, I didn't want to consider anyone else one, either. I did read a good many romance novels and enjoyed them. I just wished there were more friendship novels. That sounded like a healthier option for some people, and I definitely felt like one of those. I'd call Krichelle and Roger near the end of their workday so as not to bother them any sooner than necessary. It would be fun to play Scrabble again once I was released.

Klimczyk gave a small wave and joined Stalder in the hallway.

I turned on the television. A commercial for fast food burgers and fries appeared on the screen, followed by an ad for a new anti-depressant.

I realized I'd long since succumbed to learned helplessness, but it was difficult not to learn that lesson since we were taught it almost constantly. American culture put on an outward show of meritocracy but since the wealth gap only increased year after year, the underlying message was still that nothing we did was ever good enough, and therefore *we* must not be good enough.

Easier to blame immigrants and black people and poor folks and drag queens for our troubles.

All I could do was contribute a few dollars each month to organizations I hoped would lead others to make the changes I couldn't.

What was the emotional equivalent to anorexia, I wondered, when we tried so hard to control our failures that we dwindled away to nothing?

My eyes burned. I wondered if I should ask for a rice compress.

Perhaps it was best to try to get a little more sleep.

A nurse stopped in later to wake me and check my vitals. She handed me some meds I didn't question. And soon I was dozing again.

I awoke later feeling pressure on my hand. Afraid I was getting a new IV, I jerked my eyes open, only to find Tockner holding my non-IV hand. "How're you feeling?" he asked. He was in uniform.

Was he on duty? On his way home? Heading to work?

"Better now, P."

He smiled. I sure as hell hoped my vaccinations were still in effect. The hospital staff were all masked, but I'd sure been exposed in a dozen other ways the past twenty-four hours.

"You know," he said, "you've earned some street cred." I frowned while he continued. "I've never been shot in the line of duty. Neither have most of the other guys down at the precinct."

"A home invasion isn't exactly—"

"You were targeted because of your investigating, even if you did it half-assed."

I wasn't going to argue the point. He may well have been humoring me, but it felt sweet regardless.

"You're going to have some PTSD," Tockner went on. "We can get you some Victim Counseling through the Crime Survivor Services."

Almost made getting shot worth it.

But not the deaths of three other people.

"How do you manage to still like human beings?" I asked. "You must see far worse than I do, and it's not easy even for me."

"Well, for one thing, I don't watch detective shows."

I laughed but then winced. There was some serious bruising in addition to the gunshot wound. "What *do* you do for fun?"

He shrugged. "One of the detectives—"

"Klimczyk."

Tockner nodded. "Detective Klimczyk showed me some photos from your basement."

"Okay."

"I'd like to try out the sling one of these days."

"Anything else?"

Now he looked embarrassed, surprising after his boldness of the past couple of days.

"I like to read books." He was actually blushing.

"Why is that embarrassing?"

He shrugged again. "They're kind of kid books."

Oh my God. He wasn't a Laura Ingalls fan, too, was he?

"I'm reading a series now called *Edge of Extinction*. It's about these kids who try to outwit and survive cloned dinosaurs…"

I chuckled again, despite the pain. "Give me a few weeks to sort out the mess that is my life," I said, "and then maybe we can spend a couple of hours reading to each other."

He nodded. "Just don't tell anyone what we're doing," he said, "or *I'll* lose street cred. If anyone asks, tell them we're fucking."

P kissed me on the forehead and headed off to wherever he was going. With sleuthing hopefully forever behind me, maybe I could redirect my curiosity to finding solutions to other problems. Like how to pressure local lawmakers to fund Housing First programs. And how to develop at least a minimally satisfying social life that did not revolve around a partner.

That alone should improve my mental health.

Christmas was coming up soon. Perhaps I could purchase some German Scrabble tiles for Valentina.

I made a mental note to call Frank when I got home and set up another time to meet at the grocery. I hummed a Patrick Hernandez song toward the ceiling as a farewell to Nick. And then I nodded off to sleep once more.

Books by Johnny Townsend

Thanks for reading! If you enjoyed this book, could you please take a few minutes to write a review online? Reviews are helpful both to me as an author and to other readers, so we'd all sincerely appreciate your writing one! And if you did enjoy the book, here are some others I've written you might want to look up:

Mormon Underwear

God's Gargoyles

The Circumcision of God

Sex among the Saints

Dinosaur Perversions

Zombies for Jesus

The Abominable Gayman

The Gay Mormon Quilter's Club

The Golem of Rabbi Loew

Mormon Fairy Tales

Flying over Babel

Marginal Mormons

Mormon Bullies

The Mormon Victorian Society

Dragons of the Book of Mormon

Selling the City of Enoch

A Day at the Temple

Behind the Zion Curtain

Gayrabian Nights

Lying for the Lord

Despots of Deseret

Missionaries Make the Best Companions

Invasion of the Spirit Snatchers

The Tyranny of Silence

Sex on the Sabbath

The Washing of Brains

The Mormon Inquisition

Interview with a Mission President

Weeping, Wailing, and Gnashing of Teeth

Behind the Bishop's Door

The Moat around Zion

The Last Days Linger

Mormon Madness

Human Compassion for Beginners

Dead Mankind Walking

Who Invited You to the Orgy?

Breaking the Promise of the Promised Land

I Will, Through the Veil

Am I My Planet's Keeper?

Have Your Cum and Eat It, Too

Strangers with Benefits

What Would Anne Frank Do?

This Is All Just Too Hard

Glory to the Glory Hole!

My Pre-Bucket List

Blessed Are the Firefighters

Wake Up and Smell the Missionaries

Quilting Beyond the Rainbow

Gay Sleeping Arrangements

Queer Quilting

Racism by Proxy

Orgy at the STD Clinic

Life Is Better with Love

Please Evacuate

The Camper Killings

Recommended Daily Humanity

Let the Faggots Burn: The UpStairs Lounge Fire

Latter-Gay Saints: An Anthology of Gay Mormon Fiction (co-editor)

Available from your favorite online or neighborhood bookstore.

Wondering what some of those other books are about? Read on!

Invasion of the Spirit Snatchers

During the Apocalypse, a group of Mormon survivors in Hurricane, Utah gather in the home of the Relief Society president, telling stories to pass the time as they ration their food storage and await the Second Coming. But this is no ordinary group of Mormons— or perhaps it is. They are the faithful, feminist, gay, apostate, and repentant, all working together to help each other through the darkest days any of them have yet seen.

Gayrabian Nights

Gayrabian Nights is a twist on the well-known classic, *1001 Arabian Nights*, in which Scheherazade, under the threat of death if she ceases to captivate King Shahryar's attention, enchants him through a series of mysterious, adventurous, and romantic tales.

In this variation, a male escort, invited to the hotel room of a closeted, homophobic Mormon senator, learns that the man is poised to vote on a piece of anti-gay legislation the following morning. To prevent him from sleeping, so that the exhausted senator will miss casting his vote on the Senate floor, the escort entertains him with stories of homophobia, celibacy, mixed orientation marriages, reparative therapy, coming out, first love, gay marriage, and long-term successful gay relationships. The escort crafts the stories to give the senator a crash course in gay culture and sensibilities, hoping to bring the man closer to accepting his own sexual orientation.

Let the Faggots Burn: The UpStairs Lounge Fire

On Gay Pride Day in 1973, someone set the entrance to a French Quarter gay bar on fire. In the terrible inferno that followed, thirty-two people lost their lives, including a third of the local congregation of the Metropolitan Community Church, their pastor burning to death halfway out a second-story window as he tried to claw his way to freedom. A mother who'd gone to the bar with her two gay sons died alongside them. A man who'd helped his friend escape first was found dead near the fire escape. Two children waited outside a movie theater across town for a father and step-father who would never pick them up. During this era of rampant homophobia, several families refused to claim the bodies, and many churches refused to bury the dead. Author Johnny Townsend pored through old records and tracked down survivors of the fire as well as relatives and friends of those killed to compile this fascinating account of a forgotten moment in gay history.

The Abominable Gayman

What is a gay Mormon missionary doing in Italy? He is trying to save his own soul as well as the souls of others. In these tales chronicling the two-year mission of Robert Anderson, we see a young man tormented by his inability to be the man the Church says he should be. In addition to his personal hell, Anderson faces a major earthquake, organized crime, a serious bus accident, and much more. He copes with horrendous mission leaders and his own suicidal tendencies. But one day, he meets another missionary who loves him, and his world changes forever.

Missionaries Make the Best Companions

What lies behind the freshly scrubbed façades of the Mormon missionaries we see about town? In these stories, an ex-Mormon tries to seduce a faithful elder by showing him increasingly suggestive movies. A sister missionary fulfills her community service requirement by babysitting for a prostitute. Two elders break their mission rules by venturing into the forbidden French Quarter. A senior missionary couple try to reactivate lapsed members while their own family falls apart back home. A young man hopes that serving a second full-time mission will lead him up the Church hierarchy. Two bored missionaries decide to make a little extra money moonlighting in a male stripper club. Two frustrated elders find an acceptable way to masturbate—by donating to a Fertility Clinic. A lonely man searches for the favorite companion he hasn't seen in thirty years.

The Golem of Rabbi Loew

Jacob and Esau Cohen are the closest of brothers. In fact, they're lovers. A doctor tries to combine canine genes with those of Jews, to improve their chances of surviving a hostile world. A Talmudic scholar dates an escort. A scientist tries to develop the "God spot" in the brains of his patients in order to create a messiah. The Golem of Prague is really Rabbi Loew's secret lover. While some of the Jews in Townsend's book are Orthodox, this collection of Jewish stories most certainly is not.

The Last Days Linger

The scriptures tell us that in the Last Days, wickedness will increase upon the Earth. When leaders of the Mormon Church see a rise in the number of gay members, they believe the end is upon them. But while "wickedness never was happiness," it begins to appear that wickedness can sometimes be divine. At least, the stories here suggest that religious proscriptions condemning homosexuality have it all wrong. While gay Mormons may be no closer to perfection than anyone else, they're no further from it, either. And sometimes, being gay provides just the right ingredient to create saints—as flawed as God himself.

Mormon Madness

Mental illness can strike the faithful as easily as anyone else. But often religious doctrine and practice exacerbate rather than alleviate these problems. From schizophrenia to obsessive-compulsive disorder, from persecution complex to sexual dysfunction, autism to dissociative identity disorder, Mormons must cope with their mental as well as their spiritual health on a daily basis.

Am I My Planet's Keeper?

Global Warming. Climate Change. Climate Crisis. Climate Emergency. Whatever label we use, we are facing one of the greatest challenges to the survival of life as we know it.

But while addressing greenhouse gases is perhaps our most urgent need, it's not our only task. We must also address toxic waste, pollution, habitat destruction, and our other contributions to the world's sixth mass extinction event.

In order to do that, we must simultaneously address the unmet human needs that keep us distracted from deeper engagement in stabilizing our climate: moderating economic inequality, guaranteeing healthcare to all, and ensuring education for everyone.

And to accomplish *that*, we must unite to combat the monied forces that use fear, prejudice, and misinformation to manipulate us.

It's a daunting task. But success is our only option.

Wake Up and Smell the Missionaries

Two Mormon missionaries in Italy discover they share the same rare ability—both can emit pheromones on demand. At first, they playfully compete in the hills of Frascati to see who can tempt "investigators" most. But soon they're targeting each other non-stop.

Can two immature young men learn to control their "superpower" to live a normal life…and develop genuine love? Even as their relationship is threatened by the attentions of another man?

They seem just on the verge of success when a massive earthquake leaves them trapped under the rubble of their apartment in Castellammare.

With night falling and temperatures dropping, can they dig themselves out in time to save themselves? And will their injuries destroy the ability that brought them together in the first place?

Orgy at the STD Clinic

Todd Tillotson is struggling to move on after his husband is killed in a hit and run attack a year earlier during a Black Lives Matter protest in Seattle.

In this novel set entirely on public transportation, we watch as Todd, isolated throughout the pandemic, battles desperation in his attempt to safely reconnect with the world.

Will he find love again, even casual friendship, or will he simply end up another crazy old man on the bus?

Things don't look good until a man whose face he can't even see sits down beside him despite the raging variants.

And asks him a question that will change his life.

Please Evacuate

A gay, partygoing New Yorker unconcerned about the future or the unsustainability of capitalism is hit by a truck and thrust into a straight man's body half a continent away. As Hunter tries to figure out what's happening, he's caught up in another disaster, a wildfire sweeping through a Colorado community, the flames overtaking him and several schoolchildren as they flee.

When he awakens, Hunter finds himself in the body of yet another man, this time in northern Italy, a former missionary about to marry a young Mormon woman. Still piecing together this new reality, and beginning to embrace his latest identity, Hunter fights for his life in a devastating flash flood along with his wife *and* his new husband.

He's an aging worker in drought-stricken Texas, a nurse at an assisted living facility in the direct path of a hurricane, an advocate for the unhoused during a freak Seattle blizzard.

We watch as Hunter is plunged into life after life, finally recognizing the futility of only looking out for #1 and understanding the part he must play in addressing the global climate crisis...if he ever gets another chance.

Recommended Daily Humanity

A checklist of human rights must include basic housing, universal healthcare, equitable funding for public schools, and tuition-free college and vocational training.

In addition to the basics, though, we need much more to fully thrive. Subsidized childcare, universal pre-K, a universal basic income, subsidized high-speed internet, net neutrality, fare-free public transit (plus *more* public transit), and medically assisted death for the terminally ill who want it.

None of this will matter, though, if we neglect to address the rapidly worsening climate crisis.

Sound expensive? It is.

But not as expensive as refusing to implement these changes. The cost of climate disasters each year has grown to staggering figures. And the cost of social and political upheaval from not meeting the needs of suffering workers, families, and individuals may surpass even that.

It's best we understand that the vast sums required to enact meaningful change are an investment which will pay off not only in some indeterminate future but in fact almost immediately. And without these adjustments to our lifestyles and values, there may very well not be a future capable of sustaining freedom and democracy...or even civilization itself.

What Readers Have Said

Townsend's stories are "a gay *Portnoy's Complaint* of Mormonism. Salacious, sweet, sad, insightful, insulting, religiously ethnic, quirky-faithful, and funny."

D. Michael Quinn, author of *The Mormon Hierarchy: Origins of Power*

"Told from a believably conversational first-person perspective, [*The Abominable Gayman*'s] novelistic focus on Anderson's journey to thoughtful self-acceptance allows for greater character development than often seen in short stories, which makes this well-paced work rich and satisfying, and one of Townsend's strongest. An extremely important contribution to the field of Mormon fiction." Named to Kirkus Reviews' Best of 2011.

Kirkus Reviews

"The thirteen stories in *Mormon Underwear* capture this struggle [between Mormonism and homosexuality] with humor, sadness, insight, and sometimes shocking details....*Mormon Underwear* provides compelling stories, literally from the inside-out."

Niki D'Andrea, *Phoenix New Times*

"Townsend's lively writing style and engaging characters [in *Zombies for Jesus*] make for stories which force us to wake up, smell the (prohibited) coffee, and review our attitudes with regard to reading dogma so doggedly. These are tales which revel in the individual tics and quirks which make us human, Mormon or not, gay or not…"

A.J. Kirby, *The Short Review*

"The Rift," from *The Abominable Gayman*, is a "fascinating tale of an untenable situation…a *tour de force*."

David Lenson, editor, *The Massachusetts Review*

"Pronouncing the Apostrophe," from *The Golem of Rabbi Loew*, is "quiet and revealing, an intriguing tale…"

Sima Rabinowitz, Literary Magazine Review, *NewPages.com*

The Circumcision of God is "a collection of short stories that consider the imperfect, silenced majority of Mormons, who may in fact be [the Church's] best hope….[The book leaves] readers regretting the church's willingness to marginalize those who best exemplify its ideals: those who love fiercely despite all obstacles, who brave challenges at great personal risk and who always choose the hard, higher road."

Kirkus Reviews

In *Mormon Fairy Tales*, Johnny Townsend displays "both a wicked sense of irony and a deep well of compassion."

Kel Munger, *Sacramento News and Review*

Zombies for Jesus is "eerie, erotic, and magical."

Publishers Weekly

"While [Townsend's] many touching vignettes draw deeply from Mormon mythology, history, spirituality and culture, [*Mormon Fairy Tales*] is neither a gaudy act of proselytism nor angry protest literature from an ex-believer. Like all good fiction, his stories are simply about the joys, the hopes and the sorrows of people."

Kirkus Reviews

"In *Let the Faggots Burn* author Johnny Townsend restores this tragic event [the UpStairs Lounge fire] to its proper place in LGBT history and reminds us that the victims of the blaze were not just 'statistics,' but real people with real lives, families, and friends."

Jesse Monteagudo, *The Bilerico Project*

In *Let the Faggots Burn,* "Townsend's heart-rending descriptions of the victims...seem to [make them] come alive once more."

Kit Van Cleave, *OutSmart Magazine*

Marginal Mormons is "an irreverent, honest look at life outside the mainstream Mormon Church....Throughout his musings on sin and forgiveness, Townsend beautifully demonstrates his characters' internal, perhaps irreconcilable struggles....Rather than anger and disdain, he offers an honest portrayal of people searching for meaning and community in their lives, regardless of their life choices or secrets." Named to Kirkus Reviews' Best of 2012.

Kirkus Reviews

The stories in *The Mormon Victorian Society* "register the new openness and confidence of gay life in the age of same-sex marriage....What hasn't changed is Townsend's wry, conversational prose, his subtle evocations of character and social dynamics, and his deadpan humor. His warm empathy still glows in this intimate yet clear-eyed engagement with Mormon theology and folkways. Funny, shrewd and finely wrought dissections of the awkward contradictions—and surprising harmonies—between conscience and desire." Named to Kirkus Reviews' Best of 2013.

Kirkus Reviews

"This collection of short stories [*The Mormon Victorian Society*] featuring gay Mormon characters slammed [me] in the face from the first page, wrestled my heart and mind to the floor, and left me panting and wanting more by the end. Johnny Townsend has created so many memorable characters in such few pages. I went weeks thinking about this book. It truly touched me."

Tom Webb, *A Bear on Books*

Dragons of the Book of Mormon is an "entertaining collection....Townsend's prose is sharp, clear, and easy to read, and his characters are well rendered..."

Publishers Weekly

"The pre-eminent documenter of alternative Mormon lifestyles...Townsend has a deep understanding of his characters, and his limpid prose, dry humor and well-grounded (occasionally magical) realism make their spiritual conundrums both compelling and entertaining. [*Dragons of the Book of Mormon* is] [a]nother of Townsend's critical but affectionate and absorbing tours of Mormon discontent." Named to Kirkus Reviews' Best of 2014.

Kirkus Reviews

In *Gayrabian Nights*, "Townsend's prose is always limpid and evocative, and...he finds real drama and emotional depth in the most ordinary of lives."

Kirkus Reviews

Gayrabian Nights is a "complex revelation of how seriously soul damaging the denial of the true self can be."

Ryan Rhodes, author of *Free Electricity*

Gayrabian Nights "was easily the most original book I've read all year. Funny, touching, topical, and thoroughly enjoyable."

Rainbow Awards

Lying for the Lord is "one of the most gripping books that I've picked up for quite a while. I love the author's writing style, alternately cynical, humorous, biting, scathing, poignant, and touching.... This is the third book of his that I've read, and all are equally engaging. These are stories that need to be told, and the author does it in just the right way."

Heidi Alsop, *Ex-Mormon Foundation Board Member*

In *Lying for the Lord*, Townsend "gets under the skin of his characters to reveal their complexity and conflicts....shrewd, evocative [and] wryly humorous."

Kirkus Reviews

In *Missionaries Make the Best Companions*, "the author treats the clash between religious dogma and liberal humanism with vivid realism, sly humor, and subtle feeling as his characters try to figure out their true missions in life. Another of Townsend's rich dissections of Mormon failures and uncertainties..." Named to Kirkus Reviews' Best of 2015.

Kirkus Reviews

In *Invasion of the Spirit Snatchers*, "Townsend, a confident and practiced storyteller, skewers the hypocrisies and eccentricities of his characters with precision and affection. The outlandish framing narrative is the most consistent source of shock and humor, but the stories do much to ground the reader in the world—or former world—of the characters....A funny, charming tale about a group of Mormons facing the end of the world."

Kirkus Reviews

"Townsend's collection [*The Washing of Brains*] once again displays his limpid, naturalistic prose, skillful narrative chops, and his subtle insights into psychology...Well-crafted dispatches on the clash between religion and self-fulfillment..."

Kirkus Reviews

"While the author is generally at his best when working as a satirist, there are some fine, understated touches in these tales [*The Last Days Linger*] that will likely affect readers in subtle ways....readers should come away impressed by the deep empathy he shows for all his characters—even the homophobic ones."

Kirkus Reviews

"Written in a conversational style that often uses stories and personal anecdotes to reveal larger truths, this immensely approachable book [*Racism by Proxy*] skillfully serves its intended audience of White readers grappling with complex questions regarding race, history, and identity. The author's frequent references to the Church of Jesus Christ of Latter-day Saints may be too niche for readers unfamiliar with its idiosyncrasies, but Townsend generally strikes a perfect balance of humor, introspection, and reasoned arguments that will engage even skeptical readers."

Kirkus Reviews

Orgy at the STD Clinic portrays "an all-too real scenario that Townsend skewers to wincingly accurate proportions...[with] instant classic moments courtesy of his punchy, sassy, sexy lead character..."

Jim Piechota, *Bay Area Reporter*

Orgy at the STD Clinic is "…a triumph of humane sensibility. A richly textured saga that brilliantly captures the fraying social fabric of contemporary life." Named to Kirkus Reviews' Best Indie Books of 2022.

Kirkus Reviews

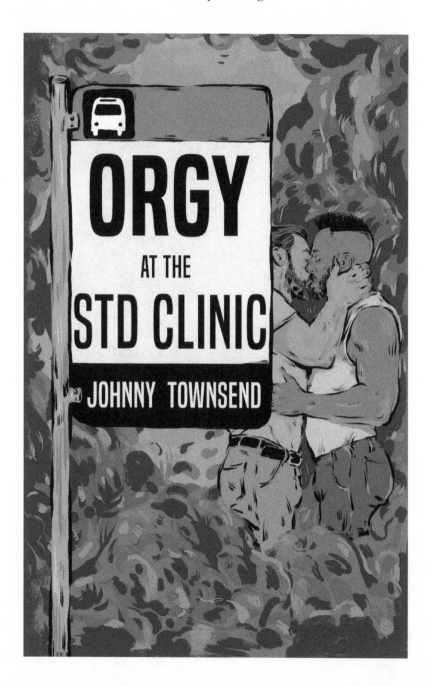

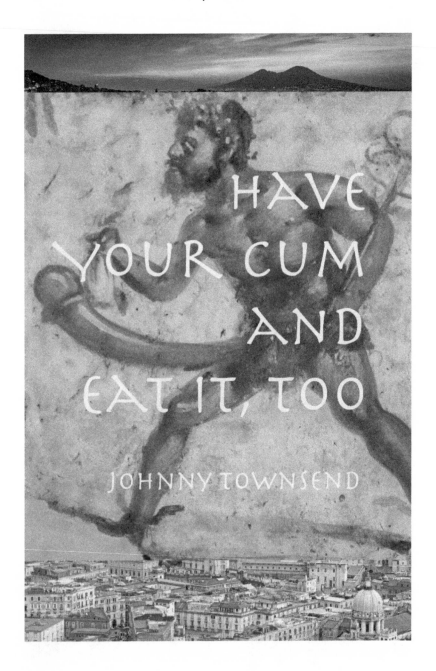

HAVE YOUR CUM AND EAT IT, TOO

JOHNNY TOWNSEND

CPSIA information can be obtained
at www.ICGtesting.com
Printed in the USA
BVHW030857270223
659294BV00005B/236